A SEEKING HEART

A Sweet Christian Romance

Aspen Valley Romance

CAROLYNE AARSEN

Chapter 1

The song had been worming through his head ever since he and Burke left the ranch.

"Untamed horses just keep running and don't ever look back."

Yet here he was, back in Aspen Valley, ready to settle down after years of living an untamed life. Running after buckles, saddles, and trophies, all dependent on eight seconds of controlling that rank bronc, hanging on.

Exciting at first. But more fearful toward the end.

Lucas parked his truck in front of the three-story brick building, one of the many along Main Street.

He paused a moment, clinging to the steering wheel of his truck, looking ahead, as if into his future.

"Um, are you okay? You look terrified." Burke, his brother, gave him a nudge from the other side of the cab of Lucas' truck.

"Just give me a minute."

"You need a paper bag? Or a shot of oxygen?"

Lucas ignored Burke's teasing but pulled in a deep breath to steady his pounding heart and ease the spinning in his head.

"You sure we should do this?" Lucas stilled the dread, déjà vu, and uncertainty all rolled into one.

"Look, it's the only land available. You want to stay? We have to take this chance."

"Potentially available," Lucas corrected.

"Don't ask, don't get. I'll head up to Aria's office to let her know we're coming. You take your time."

Thankfully his brother was sympathetic to Lucas' nervousness.

At one time, he and Aria had dated and made plans for their future. Until he broke up with her, headed for the life of freedom he had told her that he wanted.

But could he do what he and Burke had spent the past month talking about? Settle down, run the farm, and herd cows? Could he really be the cowboy he pretended to be as he raised his Smithbilt hat to the fans cheering him in the rodeo stands after a successful ride?

Even worse, could he take the chance of seeing Aria around town for the rest of his life?

Then, as he got out, the twinge in his hip and the crack of his knees reminded him that yes, he had to do this. Because the alternative was slowly wearing him down. He didn't want to end up on the arena floor, strapped to a backboard with a broken neck, his future ability to walk uncertain.

As for Aria, it would be okay. They were just kids when they were dating.

At least that's what he tried to tell himself as he hitched the belt of his jeans and walked around the truck, into the building and up the long narrow steps leading to Aria's office. Despite his brave self-talk, his heartbeat increased with each step.

The last time he and Aria had spoken was that horrible day when he told her he was leaving Aspen Valley and he wanted to break up with her. Her tears were almost his downfall, but her angry slap helped his resolve. As did the blows she landed on his shoulder with her clenched fist.

The shoulder he'd dislocated a few months previous when he got bucked off a horse while practicing in her father's arena. The intense pain seemed like an appropriate finish to their relationship.

Now, after being in town for a month, he was seeing her face to face for the first time, in her office.

He pushed down his concerns, reminded himself this was business, and pushed open the door to her office's reception area.

Burke was already inside, looking all casual and at home, his one arm resting on Louisa's desk as he chatted with Freya Porter, Aria's paralegal.

"How did Cody and his dad make out at the bull sale?" Burke asked her.

"They picked up two nice Angus bulls," Freya said, adjusting the files in her arms, her engagement ring flashing in the overhead light. "Paid a pretty penny for them."

"Not an ugly penny?"

"Har, har," she returned with a dry stare.

"So, what kind of Angus? Black? Red?"

"Red, of course. My future husband knows he doesn't need to bother with those boring blacks." Then she turned to Lucas and gave him a level glance. "Hey, there. Good to see you back, neighbor."

Lucas gave her a quick nod, sensing a retreat in her demeanor. She was all smiles with his brother, but he definitely got a different vibe from her. Her loyalties probably lay with her boss, Aria.

And not with the guy who walked away from said boss.

"It's good to be back with family. Lots of things going on in Aspen Valley."

Freya gave him an appraising look. "For sure. I hear wedding plans are in the works for Aubrey and Liam as well."

"They sure are."

"Nice they got their happy ending." Before Lucas could make a comment on that, Freya strode off down the hall to what Lucas suspected was her office.

Burke glanced from Lucas to Louisa and shivered. "Is it me, or did the temperature drop?"

"Definite chill in the air." Louisa chuckled.

"Is Aria ready for us?" Lucas asked, bringing the conversation back to the real point.

"Is anyone ever ready for you?" Louisa asked, slanting him a wry grin.

She wasn't quitting, but Lucas wouldn't give her the satisfaction of reacting to her. Instead, he gave her a bland look, repeating his question.

Louisa seemed to get the hint because she became immediately brisk and businesslike, picking up the phone and speaking to Aria.

"You can go in now," she said with a grin for Lucas.

He resisted the urge to tip his hat, thankful that she was more friendly than Freya.

"You ready?" Burke asked.

"It's just business," Lucas returned, shifting his stance and straightening his shoulders.

Burke had been the one working with Aria on a land purchase they'd had in the works. Lucas had left everything in his hands, not too keen on meeting Aria so soon after arriving in Aspen Valley.

But the people they were supposed to buy land from had changed their minds, leaving him and Burke in the lurch. However, Burke had another plan he wanted to implement, which required talking to Aria face to face.

Aria sat at her desk, but stood when they came in. She wore a pale blue sweater over a cream silk blouse, and a number of gold necklaces. Hoop earrings. Her long blonde hair hung around her face, framing it with its curls.

She's even more stunning than before, was the first thing that came to his mind.

He pushed his reaction aside as she gave Burke a smile. Then she turned to him. "Good to see you again, Lucas. It's been a while."

She sounded more relaxed than he felt and looked far more at ease.

His heart finally slowed down, and as she gestured for them to sit down, he had to suck in another breath. Just to regain his equilibrium.

"So, you said you wanted to meet with me?" she asked, glancing from Burke to Lucas. "Face to face?"

Though somehow, Lucas got the feeling that his face wasn't necessarily welcome.

"Yes," Burke said, glancing at Lucas as if to get some moral support. "We have had a wrench thrown into the works of our land deal with the Subodas."

Aria bit her lip, leaning back, her arms crossed. "Really? How?"

"Mike and Debbie called last night and said they didn't want to sell the land just yet."

Aria frowned at that. "I spoke with Mike day before yesterday. It seemed like things were moving. Slowly, mind you, but moving."

"Like I said, they just called last night."

"What reason did they give?"

"No reason. Only that they changed their minds."

"Well, that's too bad. I know their land would have worked out well for you guys. I'm sorry they let you down."

"Well, it's Lucas they are letting down more than me," Burke put in, blowing out a sigh. "But it definitely puts a damper on our expansion plans."

Burke glanced over at Lucas, as if expecting him to jump in.

But Lucas kept his expression even. Bland. Trying to look like he was more in control of his emotions than he was.

It bothered him that Aria could act so cool and collected when his own heart pounded.

"You realize this leaves us in a bind," Burke continued. "We had counted on farming that land and even bought some new equipment. I have been keeping my ear to the ground and talking to Bill Gelke at the real estate office, but there's not a lot of available land on the market."

"Have you talked to the Coffin Cheaters at the Grill and Chill?" Aria's mouth curved into a quick smile. "They seem to know what's happening before it happens."

"I chatted with Monty Bannister, but he didn't know anything either."

"Did you talk to Elyse Whittaker?" she asked. "She had told Courtney at one time that she was thinking of selling."

"I believe she has been dealing with Quinn DeVries."

At that, Aria gave Lucas a quick glance, as if wondering why he wasn't joining in.

He held her gaze a moment, but looked away, unable to keep his eyes on her.

From his seat in the office, Lucas looked out the window over Main Street. Despite the roller coaster of his feelings about the woman in the room, he had to smile. Though he had stayed away for various reasons, Aspen Valley was still the home of his best memories.

"So, to recap, you aren't buying land from Mike and Debbie and don't have anything else in mind. So, why are you here?"

This was it. Moment of truth.

Burke shot Lucas another questioning glance, but again, this was his idea, and Lucas only came along for what little moral support he could offer his brother.

"We would like you to consider selling your father's ranch. To us."

Aria's eyes widened and she sat back in her chair, as if stunned by Burke's request.

She sat so silently that Lucas was concerned Burke had pushed too hard, too fast.

"Dad's place isn't for sale," Aria said, but Lucas knew her well enough to hear that her voice lacked a strong conviction, which created a flicker of hope.

"I know it's not technically for sale," Burke put in. "But I talked to Cole, and he suggested I speak to you. I kinda got the impression he wanted to sell."

"He never said anything to me about it." Aria ran her fingers through her hair, rearranging the tidy curls. A gesture Lucas recognized all too well.

Her nervous tic. Something she did when she felt pushed into a corner.

"Of course, this is all new to me," she said. "And I'll need some time to think about it."

"But you will think about it?" Burke prompted.

The only reply he got was a tight nod.

"I know you were close to your father," Lucas finally put in, unable to keep quiet anymore. "And I know the ranch is important to you because of that. I just want you to understand that we respect that relationship."

And he truly did. Steven Waldren had been influential in helping him develop the rodeo skills that had earned him enough money to explore buying some land.

Aria didn't acknowledge his comment at first, seeming to be lost in her thoughts. But when she turned to him, her face was an expressionless mask.

"Thanks for your input," was all she said. Her voice was cool, her demeanor reserved. "I know you and my father were good friends."

Their eyes held for a measure longer than necessary and he caught a glimmer of some unnamed emotion. She flicked her gaze back to Burke.

“Like I told you, I’ll think about this," she said. Then stood, signaling the appointment was over.

Burke and Lucas stood as well.

"Thanks for your time.” Burke gave her a careful smile. "I don’t want to put you on the spot, but if you could let us know one way or the other, that would be great."

"I’ll be in touch."

"Are you coming to play practice tonight?" Burke asked, seemingly out of nowhere.

Aria looked as surprised as Lucas was at the change in topic.

"Yes, I am," she said.

"Then I’ll see you tonight," Burke said. "But I promise I won’t talk anymore about what we discussed here until you’re ready to."

"I appreciate that," Aria returned.

There was nothing more to say, so Burke and Lucas left.

When they got in the truck, Burke punched his brother on the shoulder. "You could’ve contributed something to the conversation," he admonished. "Left me flapping in the breeze there."

"Hey, this was your big plan.”

"But you’re going to be the one that will benefit from all this. I did this for you. And you thought it was a great idea until you walked into Aria’s office and stopped talking. Which is not like my usual blabbermouth brother."

Lucas didn’t try to defend himself. He was still sorting through his own response to being so close to Aria and seeing her aloof reaction to him.

"It seemed like a safe bet."

"And now?"

Lucas started the truck, glanced over his shoulder, and pulled out into Main Street.

"I dunno," he said. "I know her father has been dead five

years. She might still be grieving him, and selling the ranch would break a tie to him."

"What makes you think that?"

"Like I said in the office, she was really close to him. She was daddy's little girl. And the ranch is all she's got left of him. That would make it hard for her to let go. Especially to someone like me."

"You mean the guy who broke her heart?"

"I would say that's a little harsh, but it might be true. Which would make it even harder for her to sell the ranch, knowing that I'll be running it."

"I hope she's the forgiving sort, because if we can't expand our operations, it's going to be difficult to work you in."

Lucas nodded, knowing what was on the line for him. The farm already supported two families, and he certainly didn't come back just to work for room and board. He wanted his own place, his own land, something he could build up.

And unless Aria was willing to sell, he wasn't sure what his next step would be.

ARIA PULLED up to the community hall and turned off her car. She had to force herself to attend tonight. Work had been hectic, and after her meeting with Lucas and Burke, she felt emotionally drained.

She laid her head back against the head rest of her car, taking a breath and sending up a quick prayer. Right now, all she wanted to do was have a long soak in a bathtub, sip a glass of wine, and listen to the latest episode of her favorite podcast.

But if her father had drummed one thing into her, it was that a Waldren sticks to their commitments. At all costs.

With that reminder, she got out of the car, dragged in a calming breath, and strode across the parking lot.

As she stepped into the hall, she heard the echoing of several voices, along with some hammering going on in the background.

She thought a community play was a great idea. The proceeds would go to fixing up the ball diamonds beside the community hall.

"I thought for a moment you were bailing on us," Courtney called out as Aria approached the group by the front stage. "You were supposed to be here about twenty minutes ago."

"Busy day at the office," Aria quipped, shrugging off her oversized purse and hanging it on a hook on the wall beside the stage. "Where's Cole?"

"He's in the back room, checking out the sound system," Courtney told her. "Is something wrong? You seem upset."

Aria waved off her comment and went looking for her brother.

She found him on his hands and knees under the shelf holding the sound equipment, grumbling about wiring.

She poked him in the rear end with the toe of her boot, and he jumped, smashing his head against the shelf.

He emerged, rubbing his head, looking annoyed. "What's that all about?"

She closed the door and turned to him, arms crossed. "Why didn't you tell me you talked to Burke Prins about our land?"

Cole frowned, as if he didn't understand what she said.

"I had Burke and Lucas Prins in my office this afternoon," she continued. "Offering to buy dad's ranch. Burke said he talked to you about it."

Cole bit his lip, then nodded. "That's right, he told me that Karissa's aunt and uncle, the Subodas, were backing out of their deal. That he had talked to Grady, but there was nothing available. He found out, somehow, that I am interested in selling. I think he'd been chatting with Alistair. Great vet, but loose with the lips."

"We never talked about this." Aria tried to keep the frustration out of her voice, but all afternoon she been struggling with her seesawing emotions.

One moment she was upset with Lucas for coming back, then another moment she felt angry with herself for still feeling the old attraction. He had walked out on her, and she swore he would never hold her heart in his hands again.

Tough talk considering that all it took was one look from Lucas, and her heart went all fluttery again. It made her angry. And now she turned that frustration onto her brother, who had been wheeling and dealing behind her back.

"What do you mean we never talked about it?" Cole demanded. "Just last week you were saying we need to do something about the ranch. How it weighed you down. And if it was like that for you, how much worse for me."

Aria closed her eyes, pressing her fingers against her temples. The headache that had been threatening all afternoon was blossoming.

"We were just renting it out anyway, and now those renters are gone," Cole continued.

"I thought that after you and Courtney got married, you might want to save it for Fenna and any kids you might have together."

"Courtney's dad has enough land. We don't intend to add to it. Especially not that place."

He spat the words out, echoing the conflicted emotions that Aria had about the place she grew up.

"So do you think we should sell it?"

"Between land taxes and declaring it as extra income for both of us, renting out isn't a benefit, and neither of us want it."

Aria leaned against the desk that held a variety of sound

equipment. "So, we should do it." Her words were more of a comment than a question.

"We would have no problem getting rid of it, but Burke was the first to mention it. Wouldn't seem right to turn around and offer it to someone else."

"You realize why Burke approached you?" Aria asked.

Cole gave her a tight nod. "It's for Lucas."

"And you're okay with that?"

"Not really. But I know they're good for the money. If that's a problem for you, I can talk to Bill Gelke and have him list the property."

Aria bit her lip, destroying what little was left of her carefully applied lipstick. "Let me think about it for a while. There's no rush."

Cole was quiet, running his hand over his chin, and Aria shot him a frown. "Is there a rush?" she asked.

He shook his head, but Aria sensed something was on his mind.

"What's going on?" she pressed.

Cole hesitated, then held her questioning gaze. "Alistair wants to retire and had offered me his share of the business. Plus, Courtney and I were talking about building a house on her dad's property. The mobile home was always temporary. Fenna is getting older, and, well, I'm not supposed to say anything yet, but Courtney is expecting."

Aria just stared. Then his words registered, and she launched herself at him, throwing her arms around her brother. "That's so exciting," she squealed, hugging him tightly. She pulled back, her hands on his shoulders. "When is she due?"

"She's about three months on. She wanted to keep it quiet, but I knew you'd figure it out eventually."

"So, you have lots of reasons to need some ready cash," she said.

Cole nodded, grinning.

"Well, that makes a difference." She gave him a quick smile, shaking her head. "My brother, going to be a father."

"I already am. To Fenna." But despite that declaration, Cole's smile faltered a moment, and Aria sensed what he was thinking.

"You're a great father," she assured him. "I just know it."

"I hope so," Cole said. "There is no going back now."

"Hey, brother, when I see you with Fenna, I have absolutely no doubts."

"Thanks for that. Not going to lie. Sometimes I get worried."

Aria said nothing for a moment, acknowledging his comment. Sorting out her own history and emotions.

"Then maybe it's best that we sell the ranch. Put the past behind us and move forward."

"Are you sure?"

"I'll get there," Aria assured him, hoping emotions would follow the action. "Knowing what's at stake for you makes it easier."

"Then I'll wait until you're sure."

"Thanks for that," Aria said. "I just have to wrap my head around it all." She released a harsh laugh. "Kinda ironic to think that Lucas, who idolized our dad so much, could end up owning his ranch."

"Our ranch," Cole corrected. "Dad is long gone."

Aria gave her brother another hug. "I'm so happy for you. And for Courtney. And I promise I won't say anything to anybody."

"Not even your tight little Breakfast Club?"

"Especially not my tight little Breakfast Club," Aria said. "Brooke can't keep a secret to save her life, and Doria is way too much of a verbal processor."

"Don't I know it," Cole said. "The other day she was telling a customer something Courtney had told her. So, me and my dear bride had a chat about the things she brings up at Breakfast Club, which I don't want my vet assistant to find out."

"I wish I could say that what's said at Breakfast Club stays at Breakfast Club, but that would be a lie." Aria chuckled.

A knock on the door broke into the conversation. "Is this a secret family meeting?" Courtney asked as she stepped inside.

"You could say that," Aria replied with a wave of her hand. Then, without responding to Courtney's obvious curiosity, she walked past her into the main hall.

But as she did, she saw Burke across the room. A reminder of their visit this afternoon and who had come with him.

Her step faltered as Cole's news braided through unwelcome memories.

Had things gone the way she once wished, she and Lucas would have been married by now, and she too might be expecting a baby.

She closed her eyes a moment, banishing those recollections.

All that was behind her now. That was a dream, but now she was living reality.

Chapter 2

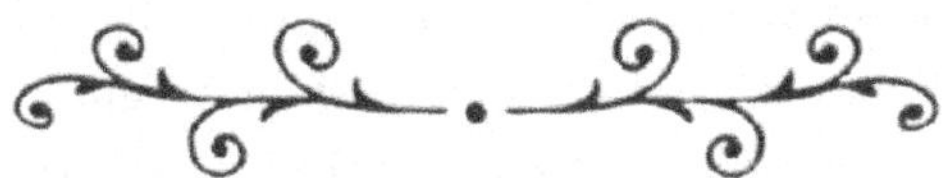

"Okay everyone, gather around," Courtney called out, holding her ever present clipboard. "There has been a glitch in our plans."

"Isn't there always?" Doria returned.

Courtney gave her a sardonic smile, then turned to people gathered around the makeshift stage set up in the hall.

"You know what this is about?" Brooke whispered to Aria.

"Just because she's my sister-in-law doesn't mean I know what's going on all the time," Aria returned.

"What's the glitch?" Karissa called out. "Please don't tell me you want to change the costumes again."

"No. Now that we've settled on the time period, that's not changing," Courtney assured her.

"I still don't know how a country western version of Pride and Prejudice is going to go over." Brooke shrugged, shaking her head.

"I heard that," Courtney called out from her place on the stage. "I think it's a fun idea, and we have a great script to work with. Unfortunately, Chloe Litman, our lead, has had a sudden epiphany. An opportunity came for her to go on a mission trip, and she decided that was more important than playing Elizabeth Bennett in a cowboy hat and boots." Courtney gave a slow shake of her head, smiling. "Priorities."

"What are we going to do?" Grady, the other lead, called out. "We've already been practicing for a couple of weeks."

"Only a couple of weeks," Courtney reiterated. "We've got a few months before the play. We're still in good shape. We just need to find someone else willing to take the role."

A tense silence fell over the crowd. Aria glanced around, noticing that every woman present did the same thing she was doing.

Not making eye contact with Courtney.

"I can see we have a stampede of volunteers to take this on," Courtney joked. "Come on ladies, help me out here. It's not that big a deal."

"Says you," Brooks called out. "This is definitely a chance for complete public humiliation. And I don't know anyone who would want to take that on. And don't even think about me. I'm taking care of hair and makeup."

"I know, Brooke. But we need an Elizabeth. And seeing as we have no volunteers, I'm exerting my rights as a dictator director, and volunteering someone myself," Courtney said. "Aria, you would be perfect as Elizabeth."

Aria stared at her, open-mouthed. This was the second time today she had been caught flat-footed.

"No way," she insisted, waving the comment off. "I'm not taking this on. I'm perfectly happy as one of the Bennet sisters."

"And miss out on your chance for fame and fortune? And the opportunity to star opposite Grady?" Courtney teased.

"I think Aria would make an excellent Lizzie Bennett," Grady put in with a wink Aria's way.

Aria wasn't sure what to make of that. When she first moved back, she and Grady had gone on a couple of dates, but she didn't feel any sparks. And she got the impression

Grady felt the same. They had become good friends, and that seemed to suit them both.

But starring in a semi-romantic play with him?

Courtney gave Aria what she knew was her "*I'm not quitting*" look. Aria had been on the other end of that look many times growing up.

Courtney wanted her to go riding.

Courtney wanted her to help build the treehouse.

Courtney wanted Aria to tell her brother Cole how much she loved him.

She would give Aria "the look," and Aria knew her friend wasn't quitting until she got her way.

Aria glanced around the room, looking for a likely prospect. "How about Karissa? She'd make a great Elizabeth."

"Already busy with the costumes," Karissa returned, giving Aria a complacent grin.

"What about Shelby?"

"She's pregnant."

"Isn't there a name for that kind of prejudice?" Aria returned. "Babyist or something? I'm sure I read about a lawsuit over that very issue in law school."

"I'm sure you're making that up." Courtney clutched her clipboard close, a sure sign she was digging in for the long haul.

Aria shot another look around the gathering, but no one made eye contact.

"You've got a splendid memory," Courtney pressed Aria. "You know the part. I've seen you helping Chloe with her lines."

Aria felt her resolve weakening, as it always did with her friend.

"Please? We need you. Western Pride and Prejudice needs you. Aspen Valley Theatrical Society needs you."

"Please, Aria," Burke added, followed by a few more people.

"Fine. Fine." Aria threw up her hands in surrender. "I'll be your Elizabeth. But only because you won't leave me alone until it happens."

"Never seen anyone so reluctant for their stab at fame and fortune."

"Wait. Fortune? We're getting paid?" Grady asked with a hopeful tone.

"You wish. The fortune is in public good will. Here's your copy of the script," Courtney said, coming down from the stage, handing Aria a thick envelope. "I've highlighted your lines and stage directions."

Aria held Courtney's now bland gaze. "You owe me."

Courtney just grinned back. "Put it on the tab." Then she turned back to the assembled gathering. "Okay, people. Just a reminder. Starting next week, we're doing two practices a week. Tuesday and Thursdays. We've only got a couple of months until show time. All right. Let's do this. Let's have some fun."

Aria wasn't sure she would call this fun, but then she pulled out the script and turned to the first page.

"It is a truth universally acknowledged, that a single man in possession of a good fortune must be in want of a wife."

Despite her annoyance with Courtney, Aria smiled at the first lines of the book, which had been included in the script. Pride and Prejudice was the first adult book she had taken out of the library, so it held a special place in her heart. She loved Elizabeth's spunkiness and how Mr. Darcy put aside the utter chaos of the Bennet family and fell in love with Elizabeth for herself.

The door of the hall flew open, the wind outside slamming it against the wall.

"Sorry. Sorry," a deep voice called out.

Aria's heart plunged down to the floor.

Really? Lucas?

Again?

Don't turn around. Don't make eye contact.

But despite her better judgement, she shot a quick look back.

Just in time to see him looking directly at her.

She wished she didn't flush as she glanced away. Wished those girlish feelings for him didn't come creeping back around the edges of her heart.

You're a professional lawyer, she reminded herself. *He's just a cowboy.*

She pulled in a deep breath, lifted her chin, and walked over to Grady.

"Well, Mr. Darcy, I guess we'll be working together," she declared, affecting an English accent as she held out her hand.

Grady grinned at her, took it, turned it, then kissed the back of it, sweeping down in a half bow. "It will be my pleasure, I'm sure, Miss Bennet." He gave her a wink, and she felt a flash of relief.

Working with Grady should work out just fine.

"YOU COULD HAVE TOLD me Aria was involved in the play," Lucas grumbled as he took the wrench from Burke.

"What difference would that have made?" Burke squatted down, level with the bottom of the tractor. "What do you figure we should do?"

"It needs a new hydraulic hose," Lucas muttered, giving the nut a twist.

"That's not a big problem."

"I didn't say it was." He pushed himself along on the dolly.

"You sound like it is."

Lucas just grunted as he worked the other nut loose, then

pulled the leaking hose off. Of course, he got hydraulic fluid all over his pants. Of course, they were his last clean pair.

He pulled himself out from under the tractor, grabbed the hose, and stood.

Burke leaned against the tire of the tractor, arms crossed, giving him a wry look.

"What?" Lucas coiled up the old hose and brought it to the counter.

"You sound grumpy."

Lucas just shook his head. "Not grumpy at all. Just don't enjoy doing mechanic work with an audience."

"You sound like dad. I remember him always telling us that this wasn't a spectator sport."

Lucas laughed at the memory, which was immediately followed by a twinge of grief. Though their parents had been gone for five years, he still missed them. Even more now that he was spending every day at the ranch.

"Unless you have anything else for me to fix, I'll head to town to get a new hose," Lucas said.

Burke held his gaze. "You're sure about this? Settling down here in Aspen Valley?"

"Of course I am." Lucas shot him another frown. "Why? Are you changing your mind?"

"No way. I'm glad you're back here. You've always been restless, and I know how much the rodeo life meant to you."

"I'm not bailing on you," Lucas protested. "I'm sticking around." He didn't want to feel annoyed, but the challenging note in his brother's voice frustrated him.

And niggled at the questions that had more to do with Aria than with sticking around.

"I'm heading out now," Lucas said. "If you need anything, let me know."

Burke nodded, pushing himself away from the tractor tire, then frowned as he glanced at his phone. "Shoot, I forgot. I promised Roxie that I'd pick her up from physio." He blew out a breath, then looked over at Lucas. "You're in town. Can you pick her up?"

"Sure. What time?"

"She's done at about noon."

"That could work out. Hopefully the hose should be ready by then."

"If you need help to put it back on, let me know."

Lucas grinned at him as he wrapped the hose in an old towel. "Like you helped me take it off?"

"Moral support is underrated." Burke gave him another grin, then sauntered off, whistling.

Lucas watched him go, trying not to feel a tinge of envy at his brother's happiness. It was good to see him and Karissa together. In fact, every time he drove into town and saw their names still painted on the bridge, he had to grin.

Remnants of high school.

Twenty minutes later, he sat in the waiting room of Patrice Anderson's physio studio, reading an old National Geographic magazine. Calling it reading was a stretch. Mostly he just glanced at the beautiful pictures.

He looked up just as Roxie came down the open hallway, walking carefully, wincing as she did so.

Patrice was right behind her, holding a folder that she set on the receptionist's table. "I made some notes," she said to the older woman sitting behind the desk. "Can you input them into her file?"

The woman, who Lucas didn't recognize, nodded, but before she turned back to her computer, she gave Lucas a careful smile.

Patrice looked from her receptionist to Lucas and shook her head, her auburn hair shining in the overhead lights. "Burke warned me you were a charmer."

"Warned you?" Lucas stood, setting the magazine aside as Roxie slung her backpack over one arm. The bruises had faded from her face, but he could still see the faint scars from the accident she and RayAnn had been in several weeks ago. "Why would he do that?"

"Not sure."

Patrice turned back to Roxie. "I need to emphasize how important regular stretching and exercise is for your leg," she reminded his sister.

Roxie just shrugged; resistance stamped on her face. His younger twin sisters weren't known for their meekness. Especially not Roxie, the bossier of the two girls.

"I'm going out to the truck," Roxie said, her voice holding a tone of resentment.

Oh boy. She was in a mood. It was going to be a real fun trip back to the ranch.

He was about to follow her when Patrice touched his arm. "Can I talk to you a moment?" she asked.

"Sure." He had time. The machine shop had called to say that the hose wouldn't be ready for another hour.

He followed her down the hall, and she turned into a small room, but didn't close the door.

She leaned back against the padded table behind her, folding her arms, looking like she was ready for a serious chat. "How much pull do you have with your sister?"

"Don't know as anyone ever did with the R's," he said, blowing out a sigh.

"R's?"

"Yeah. Roxie and RayAnn. Both R. The R's." Lucas shrugged. "A family nickname."

"Cute. Well, this R needs to focus on the exercises I gave her. She's losing mobility, and that's not a good thing at her age. It will only get worse, not better."

"What do you want me to do?"

"Encourage her to do her exercises. Remind her what's at stake."

"Which is?"

"I can only say so much because of patient confidentiality,

though she told me she didn't care what I told to whom." Patrice shook her head, telegraphing her discontent. "But I can say that if she doesn't do what I've asked her to do, she will be limping when she's in her twenties and potentially looking at early onset osteoarthritis."

Lucas felt a tiny shiver down his spine at Patrice's words. Same thing he'd been warned about the last time he got dumped off a horse and ended up in the hospital. The doctor who had looked at his x-rays gave him the same song and dance about osteoarthritis.

That was one of the reasons he'd quit rodeo. There wasn't enough money or enough glory to end up incapacitated.

"Okay, I'll see what I can do." Lucas gave her a careful smile. Patrice was pretty. He guessed he was maybe a couple of years older than her. Her auburn hair and faint smattering of freckles gave her an approachable air.

Way more approachable than his ex-girlfriend, with her designer clothes and perfect makeup.

But he felt nothing more than a simple acknowledgement of her potential appeal.

To someone else.

"I appreciate that." Patrice blew out a sigh, glancing at her watch.

"Before you leave, why don't you print out the exercises she needs to do so I know for myself what has to happen."

"That would be great."

She gave him another smile, then strode out of the room.

A few minutes later, Lucas climbed into the truck, the paper Patrice had given him folded up and shoved in the back pocket of his blue jeans.

"She give you her phone number?" Roxie mocked as he turned the truck on. "Is that what's on that paper?"

"Of course she did," Lucas returned as he pulled onto the street. "I'm irresistible."

"My friends think you're pretty hot."

"Your friends need to get their eyes checked."

Roxie just shrugged as Lucas drove toward Main Street.

"Where are we going? This isn't the way home."

"I've got an hour to kill before I have to pick up my hose. I thought we could go to the Pasta Place. Catch up with Aubrey. Haven't seen her for a while."

Roxie slouched down in her seat, biting at her thumbnail. "Do we have to?"

"Or we could park ourselves in front of the machine shop and you could check your messages or whatever keeps you staring at your phone all day while I wait."

"That sounds indescribably boring."

"And I'm sure you would let me know with sighs too deep for words." Lucas pulled into the closest empty parking spot. "Pasta Place it is."

"What about the Grill and Chill?" Roxie asked.

"Nah. I'm in the mood for some ravioli."

He got out of the truck and waited for his sister. She grimaced as she took a few steps.

"Physio extra hard on you today?" he asked, coming to her side and offering his arm.

"I was just about crying. And then she did some acupuncture. I thought I was going to die, it hurt so much."

"I've had that done," Lucas sympathized. "It can be super painful."

Roxie took his outstretched arm, leaning heavily on him as they walked. Either she was in an intense amount of pain, or she was dawdling, putting off seeing Aubrey again.

Lucas guessed at his sister's reluctance. Aubrey had been involved in the same accident that had injured Roxie.

Initially, Roxie had blamed Aubrey, but then the truth had come out. Roxie was the one at fault. It had been a tough lesson for his sister. And now Aubrey's engagement to their brother Liam had created a strained situation for Roxie and RayAnn.

Aubrey had told Roxie that she had forgiven her, that she wasn't holding it against her, but Roxie's own guilt weighed on the young girl's shoulders.

In fact, that lie had created a lot of problems for both girls. RayAnn, who had held up Roxie's lie, was doing community service at the local Food Bank and helping with the community play as a consequence.

Roxie helped out at the Family and Community Support Services, taking care of children after school while their mothers worked. She had bemoaned the fact that while RayAnn had time to work part-time at the movie theatre, Roxie had yet to find a job that she could do.

Lucas held open the door for Roxie and stood aside as she slowly made her way inside.

Seriously. A slug could get inside faster than her.

But he kept holding the door, stifling his comments.

Finally, she was inside, and he helped her to the nearest table.

"This place smells funny," Roxie grumbled, shifting in her seat.

"It's making my mouth water." Lucas looked around. The restaurant was full except for an empty table right beside them. Nice for his future sister-in-law that things were going so well.

The restaurant had a fresh decor since Aubrey had taken it over from her father. Plants hung along one wall, and large windows let an abundance of light into the place.

Roxie didn't reply to his comment. She just pouted and pulled her phone out.

A few moments later, Aubrey approached their table, all smiles as she set glasses of water and menus in front of them. "Well hello, you guys. Nice to have you here."

There wasn't even the smallest trace of condemnation in Aubrey's voice. In fact, she seemed happy to see Roxie.

"I didn't know you were working today," Lucas responded,

looking puzzled to see her. "I thought you taught Taekwondo on Saturday mornings."

"The next group doesn't start for a couple of weeks. I thought I would help my dad in the meantime. He's still looking for someone to help out." Aubrey's gaze darted to Roxie, as if dropping a very large hint.

"Just Saturdays?" Lucas clarified.

"Just Saturday mornings."

He glanced over at Roxie, who wasn't looking up, her gaze intent on her phone, her fingers flying over the letters on the bottom. Texting. Probably grumbling with either RayAnn or her friends.

Aubrey waited a moment, as if giving Roxie an opportunity to say something, then turned to Lucas.

"I'll be back to take your order. Do you want anything else to drink for now?"

"Just some coffee, please."

"Coming up."

She walked away, and Lucas leaned across the table, getting closer to his sister. "Why are you so rude?"

Roxie pressed her lips together, her fingers still. Then she swallowed as she swiped at her face.

"Hey, what's wrong?"

His sister sniffed and dug into her backpack, pulling out an old handkerchief. Lucas' heart folded as he recognized the pattern.

"Is that one of Dad's old hankies?" he asked, his voice quiet.

She nodded, then wiped her face. "I found it when me and Shelby cleaned out their bedroom. I asked if I could keep it." She looked down at it, then eased out a heavy sigh. "I miss them."

"Oh sweetie, I understand." He wanted to say that he missed them too, but didn't want to take away from Roxie's grief. She had only been twelve when their parents passed away so suddenly and tragically. Old enough to have many fond memories and too young to be left an orphan.

Shelby had done her best to take care of the twins and their younger brother Jacob after their parents' deaths, but it wasn't the same as having a mother and father.

He was quiet a moment, reaching across the table to cover his sister's hand. "It's not the same, but you know you've got me and Burke and Shelby and Klint and Karissa and Liam all looking out for you girls and Jacob. And believe it or not, Aubrey as well. I think she would like to offer you a job. I know you said you wanted to earn some extra money for college."

Roxie bit her lip again, folding and unfolding the handkerchief on the table. "I can't work here. I've got community service."

"But that's only during the week. This would be Saturdays. And you'd probably get tips."

Roxie looked up at him, her eyes filling with tears again. "How am I supposed to wait on tables when I can hardly walk?"

Did she set herself up on purpose? Because this was the perfect opportunity to follow through on what Patrice said.

He reached back, pulled the paper out of his pocket, and laid it on the table.

"Patrice didn't give me her phone number like you thought. These are the exercises she's been after you to do."

Roxie frowned at the paper. "Why did she bug you about that?"

"Because she's concerned that you aren't doing what you're supposed to do."

This got him another glare. "So, you were talking about me behind my back?"

"Well, not technically. You were in my truck. And I believe it was facing north-"

"You know what I mean. I don't know why she cares."

Lucas grew serious. "Roxie, she cares because it matters to her that you get the most benefit from what she's doing with you. She doesn't want to see you hobbling around when you could be much stronger. And I care because I've been injured, and I've had to do physio. I know what a difference it's made for me."

Roxie leaned her head back against the chair of the booth. "But it's so much work."

Again, Lucas pushed down his irritation with his sister, reminding himself that she was young, and she was struggling.

"I don't know why Aubrey would even want to hire me," she continued. "Especially after what me and RayAnn..." her voice broke again, and Lucas gave her hand a gentle squeeze.

"Especially because of what you said about the accident?"

"I shouldn't have lied about it," she admitted, sniffing. "Made it sound like it was her fault. Aubrey is so nice to me when she should be angry, and I feel horrible and don't deserve to get better."

Lucas felt like a light bulb had gone on.

He waited a moment, letting her comment settle, then squeezed her hands again. "Of course you deserve to get better. And you need to know we all want the best for you and want to help you. Patrice, me, the rest of the family. Your in-laws. Aubrey."

"I feel like such a horrible person. I feel so guilty, and I just want it to go away."

He couldn't help a soft smile at her admission.

"That makes me think of a quote. 'Only good people feel guilt.'"

"What does that mean?"

"If you didn't feel bad about what you did, I would be worried more. It would mean it doesn't matter to you. I think what you need to do is let Aubrey be nice to you. Maybe take the job and do the best you can until you get better. Work on healing yourself. Move on and learn."

As he spoke the words, he realized that what he said could apply to himself.

The guilt he felt when he saw Aria. The feeling that he had let her down in such a bad way.

But what else could he have done?

It had been the right choice, no matter how it hurt her.

Chapter 3

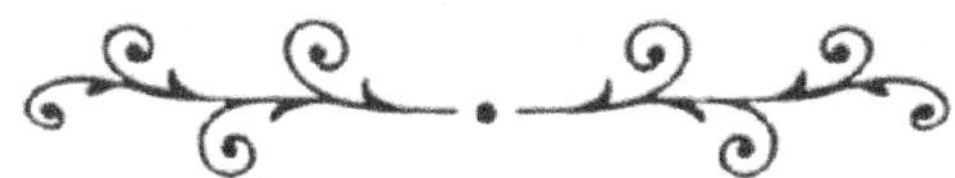

Aria parked beside her brother's car in the parking lot of the hall and sat back in the seat. Right now, she didn't want to go inside. Her day had been a whirlwind of busyness, and in the middle of it all, Cole had called her to ask if she'd had time to think about selling the ranch. Neither of them was living there, or wanted to live there, and if Cole needed the money, it was probably a good idea.

But to sell it to Lucas?

She slowed her breathing, praying with each breath. Slowly, she felt on top of her emotions.

Until a truck pulled up in front of the hall, and Lucas Prins stepped out. He wore his cowboy hat, a denim jacket, and faded blue jeans.

As he walked around the back of the truck, she noticed his ever-present cowboy boots.

She remembered teasing him about them. Saying he'd never be able to run in those. He always retorted that he didn't need to run when he had a horse to do the running for him.

He opened the tailgate just as the passenger door opened and one of the twins stepped out.

Aria guessed that Roxie was still limping from the way she sauntered up the walk. As Lucas followed her, Aria's mind sifted back to the conversation she'd overheard at The Pasta Place.

Lucas encouraging his sister to continue with her therapy. How much support she had from the family. Listening to him talking to Roxie had shifted her perception of him.

Had softened her heart toward him.

Another breath, another struggle to dismiss any feelings about him at all.

It annoyed her that all he had to do was show up in Aspen Valley for her to feel this disjointed. She'd endured so much more than a broken heart when he left.

She dug her lipstick out of her purse, pulled her rear-view mirror down, and outlined her lips. Pressed them together. Looked closer.

Perfect. She finger combed her hair, loose curls falling over her shoulders, straightened her blazer, then stepped out of the car.

As she did, another car pulled up beside her, and Courtney got out, slinging a messenger bag over her shoulder.

"Hey, you," Courtney called out. "Where did you just come from?"

"Work?" Aria frowned at her. "Why do you ask?"

Courtney gestured to her own blue jeans and faded hoodie. "You trying to make the rest of us look bad?" she teased.

"If I'm going to be a leading lady, I may as well dress the part." Aria kept her tone light, even though Courtney's teasing created the usual niggle of disquiet about how she looked. Too much? Not suitable?

Trying too hard?

"Well, you certainly look Instagram-ready."

"I don't even use Instagram," Aria returned as Courtney

joined her, and together, they walked up the wooden stairs into the hall.

"You should. You could give us peasants hair and make-up tips."

Aria was about to reply to that when someone called out Courtney's name and with a quick wave of her hand, she was off.

The hall buzzed with activity. In one corner she saw Burke, Liam, Klint, and Lucas sitting on sawhorses, chatting and laughing. RayAnn joined them, and Aria sensed from the girl's blush and the laughter of the men that they were poking fun of the her. When she punched Lucas in the shoulder, Aria knew for sure.

But RayAnn didn't look angry.

And when Lucas pulled her to his side in a half-hug, RayAnn put her head on his shoulder.

The sight twisted Aria's heart, resurrecting memories. The Prins family was a busy, noisy family that she had loved spending time with when she and Lucas were dating.

Aria spun around on her high heels, almost losing her balance but thankfully regaining it as she strode to the stage and sat down. She pulled her script out of the briefcase and flipped it to the scene they would be rehearsing.

"Hey Aria, how's the lines coming?" Grady sat down beside her, holding his own script.

"This has given me a new appreciation for actors," she admitted. "How to memorize lines, then not deliver them like they're memorized. A tricky balance."

"I hear yah. Courtney said we'd have cue cards in case we get stuck."

"I know, but I don't want to be staring over your shoulder when I'm supposed to be declaring undying love for you and staring into your eyes."

"That's in the script?" Grady flipped through the pages, and Aria put her hand on his to stop him.

"I'm kidding."

"I kind of thought you were," he returned with a grin. "Refresh my memory, we're doing the first scene tonight."

"Yeah. Courtney called and told me she wanted me to feel comfortable right from the get-go. She said you'd only gotten to the second scene anyway."

"Good idea." Grady fiddled with the pages, biting his lip.

"You're still okay with me taking over from Chloe?" The last thing she needed was tension between herself and the leading man.

Grady waved away her question. "That's not a problem at all. I think you'll make a much better Elizabeth Bennet. And, let's be honest, you are one of the prettiest girls in town."

"According to the play, that should have me playing Jane," Aria teased. "After all, the script says that Mr. Darcy only found me tolerable compared to Jane and only gave Elizabeth the benefit of her fine eyes."

"Well, you do also have very fine eyes." Grady gave her a gentle smile and then grew serious. "Speaking of fine eyes…" his voice trailed off, and he rolled his script up, tapping it on his knees. "I need some advice in matters of the heart."

"Different parts of the body, but sure…?" Aria pulled back, hoping Grady wasn't reviving their old relationship.

"I want to ask a girl out. Sorry. It's not you."

"No apology necessary. I didn't think it was."

"Trouble is, I'm not sure she'd be interested." Grady sighed, his tapping increasing.

"So, why don't you ask her out?" she encouraged.

"I'm don't know if she'd say yes."

This surprised Aria. Grady always seemed so self-confident. So self-contained. In fact, that was one struggle they'd had when they dated. Aria kept her cards close to her chest, but so did Grady.

Not a great combination for intimacy.

Aria moved closer, lowering her voice. "You won't know if you won't ask her."

"Well…it's complicated."

"So, who is she?"

Grady blew out his breath on a sigh. "Brooke Dillon."

"Really? Brooke?"

"Shush. Not so loud." Grady bopped her with his script, frowning at her. "I haven't even talked to her yet."

"Why not?"

"You've been around Aspen Valley long enough to know that Brooke only has eyes for George Bamford. I don't know how many times I've come to the Grill and Chill to see her just staring at him. Chatting him up."

Aria resisted the urge to roll her eyes. She knew what Grady spoke of. She'd often seen the same thing. She'd tried to urge Brooke to consider letting go of her obsession. Maybe Grady asking her out would help her to see other options. Realize George wasn't exactly the catch of the day. Or year. Or however long she'd been obsessed about the guy.

"Talk to her," she encouraged. "Keep it simple. If it's any consolation, I had lunch with her yesterday at The Pasta Place instead of George's Grill and Chill. So that's growth."

They had lunch at the same time Lucas Prins was encouraging his younger sister. The memory of that conversation resurrected another pang of sorrow she was growing tired of.

Why did his rejection still bother her?

She'd gotten over many other disappointments and griefs. Lucas was part of her childish past.

"I guess that's a positive."

Aria pulled her attention away from Lucas, who she could hear laughing with his younger sister, joking with Burke as they dragged lumber around for the sets.

"You know, we could set something up," Aria said. "Why don't I ask Brooke to go with me for lunch this week, and you could just so happen to be stopping in. I'll ask you to join us. You can take it from there."

Grady nodded slowly, as if thinking about it. "That sounds like a plan."

"It's a splendid plan. We could do it a few more times, and then she'll start wondering why you're stopping by, and I could tell her."

Even as she laid out her ideas, she had to smile. This was like junior high all over again. Passing notes from a friend to her friend's crush. Setting up secret meetings.

"Look, Grady, even though things didn't work out between us, you're a great guy," she encouraged. "Just a wonderful person. Head and shoulders above George, that's for sure."

Then Grady smiled at her. "Thanks for pep talk, though I think me and George are the same height."

"Trust me, I know this for sure. Believe in yourself."

Grady chuckled at that. "Listen to you getting all sentimental and rah, rah. You're usually so serious and wary."

"Sorry. Product of my environment."

She threw the comment out as a joke, but Grady's expression grew serious. "You've said that before. I wish you would tell me a bit more about that environment."

Aria looked down at her papers, pressing her lips together and shook her head. "You know that's off-limits."

"I do."

Her reluctance to talk about her past was one of the sticking points between them.

But then he slipped his arm across her shoulders and pulled her toward him in a sideways hug. "Thanks for the push. Let me know when you're going, and I'll be there."

"Just show up, be yourself."

She laid her head just for a moment on his shoulder, enjoying the moment of connection. Letting herself wish, once again, that things could have worked out with this very kind, uncomplicated man.

Just then, Lucas walked past them, his grey eyes piercing, as if trying to figure out what they were talking about.

She held his gaze, determined not to let him intimidate her.

Despite her resolve, however, a tiny shiver of awareness trickled down her spine.

She turned back to Grady, forcing a smile. "Guess we should try running some lines before rehearsal," she suggested, bringing things back to the practical.

"Sure. Sounds good."

But even as they traded lines, Aria felt as if a part of her was aware of precisely where Lucas was each time he looked over at her.

"AND SCENE." Aria did a mock curtsey toward Grady, flipping her hand toward him in what looked to Lucas like a flirtatious gesture.

It shouldn't have bothered him as much as it did.

Seeing her all cozy with Grady at the beginning of practice created a low-level annoyance he had no right to feel.

But still.

"Excellent. Well done, you guys." Courtney came forward with her ever-present clipboard, but she was frowning. "Only one criticism. Grady, you seem to deliver your lines like you're reciting a grocery list."

"That's impossible," Grady returned, shooting her a grin. "I don't make grocery lists. I just go into the store and let adventure take over."

"Maybe you should let adventure take over when you're reading your lines."

"I'll try." Grady looked down at his script and heaved a theatrical sigh. "Oh, the life of an up-and-coming Broadway star."

Courtney and everyone around chuckled, but Lucas didn't think it funny.

"Let's take a break and start again in twenty minutes," Courtney announced.

Lucas brushed the sawdust off his pants, then pulled his leather gloves off and tucked them into the back pocket of his jeans.

He walked over to the table, poured himself some coffee and then joined Cole at the back corner of the hall.

"How are the sets coming along?" Courtney asked as she sat by him.

"I'm just the worker," Lucas returned, taking a sip of his coffee. "Ask Burke. He's the brains behind my brawn."

"As long as you want no more changes, we should be okay." Burke joined them, dropping into a chair beside Lucas. RayAnn sat across from them, wiping her hands with an old rag.

"You've got paint all over you." Lucas reached across the table to wipe a spot off her nose.

RayAnn jerked back, frowning at him.

"What's your deal, grumble pants?" Lucas asked.

She just sighed, pressing her lips together, and for a moment Lucas didn't think his chatty sister would say anything.

Then she leaned closer, her lip curled in disgust. "My deal is, I don't have time for my friends anymore. I'm busy all the time. And I'm tired."

"You know why you have to do this, right?" Burke put in.

RayAnn blew out a heavy sigh. "I know. But still. I didn't think community service would be this much work."

"It's not supposed to be fun," Lucas reminded her.

RayAnn looked up and waved to Aria. "Come and sit here," she called out, pulling out the empty chair beside her.

Lucas saw Aria hesitate, but then she forced a smile and joined them.

RayAnn and Roxie were only seven when he and Aria broke up, but lately they'd both mentioned her a few times. Asked him if he and Aria would ever get back together again.

Conversation Lucas usually nipped in the bud.

But he knew Aria fascinated both girls. Her grace, her style. Her exotic good looks.

"You're a talented actress," RayAnn observed as Aria sat down. "It's fun to watch you."

"That's encouraging." Aria gave her a quick smile. "I feel like I'm kind of stumbling along."

"I think you're doing great. Too bad you have to act with Grady."

"I heard that," Grady warned, settling down at the far end of the table.

Lucas gave RayAnn a kick under the table, but when Aria's head shot up and she jerked back, he realized he'd connected with the wrong leg.

"So sorry," he apologized. "That was my fault. I was trying to be diplomatic."

"Did you just kick Aria?" RayAnn asked, shocked.

"Can you say that louder?" Lucas frowned at her. "Yes. By mistake. I was aiming for you. You don't need to talk about Grady like that."

"Trouble is, she's right." Grady sighed. "I feel like I'm already at the top of my game here." Then he looked over at Lucas, grinning. "You're a natural ham, Prins. Why don't you take over?"

"Not a chance. I'm not putting myself in front of people to be ridiculed."

"That would only happen if you do a lousy job," RayAnn commented. "And I think you'd make a great Mr. Darcy."

Lucas shot her a warning glance, surprised at her cheerleading, but she didn't seem to notice. Instead, she was now looking at Aria. "Don't you think he'd make a good Mr. Darcy?"

"Stop creating dissension in the ranks," Courtney put in, saving Aria from having to answer. "Grady does a great job of being Mr. Darcy."

"You said he sounds like he's reciting a grocery list," RayAnn returned.

Burke leaned forward, putting a warning hand on his sister's hand. "Sweetie, your opinion can matter," he said, lowering his voice. "But not now."

RayAnn jerked her hand away from his and sat back, frowning.

"I think Grady is doing just fine," Courtney continued.

"Yeah, I suppose, but he's no cowboy. Not like Lucas." RayAnn insisted, with a toss of her head.

Lucas wished she would stop, but she was out of reach of his foot now.

"Yeah, Lucas is the real deal," Grady agreed, nursing his cup of coffee. "I can wear the hat and the boots, but you're right, RayAnn, I'm an accountant. Not a cowboy."

"Technically, I'm not a genuine cowboy, either." Lucas gave him a quick grin. "I just play one every time I get on a crazy horse and try to hang on."

"Whatever made you start on that path?" Grady asked.

Lucas tried not to glance Aria's way, thinking about her father, wondering if talking about him would bother her. It sure seemed like it when they were in her office last week.

"Steven Waldren got me interested in bronc riding. Don't know if you know this, but he used to be quite a name in the rodeo circuit. He won lots of championships. He had an arena on his place, and I would stop in when..." he paused, taking a moment.

When he was dating Aria.

"He held a couple of clinics," Lucas continued before anyone could follow through on his pause. "And I loved watching him work with the horses and the other cowboys. He caught me watching once and invited me to take part. I tried a couple of times, and he seemed to think I had a knack for it."

Again, another look Aria's way to judge how she was taking all this.

She was looking down at her mug, but he could see from the tightness around her mouth that the conversation bothered her.

"And then you started rodeoing?" Grady asked, seeming to be genuinely interested.

"Not all at once. I competed in smaller ones, did okay, won a few trophies, then slogged my way up to bigger ones in the circuit."

"So, how do you practice something like that? Keep trying until you don't fall off and hope you don't break every bone in your body in the meantime?"

"Not really. I got tips from Steven. He had a friend who was a stock contractor, and he'd lend some of his easier saddle broncs. We would practice on them. But we did other exercises on the ground, which primed us to create muscle memory."

"Like what?"

"He had a spur board we'd practice spurring on. He'd make us work on our form sitting in the saddle whenever we could. He had a couple of older saddle horses who were okay with all the movement we'd make, recreating the spurring and leaning we'd do." Lucas chuckled. "I don't know how many times he nagged at me to watch my mark out."

"Mark out?"

He was about to reply, but then Aria put in, "Means the rider is touching the bronc's shoulders with both feet on its first jump out of the chute."

Her comment surprised him, but not her knowledge. Lucas remembered her watching while he practiced. Obviously, she'd heard her father call out enough times for her to remember his instruction.

He sent a quick glance her way, and for a heartbeat, their eyes held.

Once again, the old attraction simmered, but he pushed it down.

Hopefully with time and seeing her enough, that would dissipate.

"Yeah, most everything I learned about saddle bronc riding I learned from Steven Waldren. I admired him. I miss him too."

He glanced at Aria, wondering how this talk of her father affected her. But she took a quick sip of her coffee, pushed her chair away, and left the table.

Lucas watched her go, feeling bad for her.

She probably missed her father as well.

Chapter 4

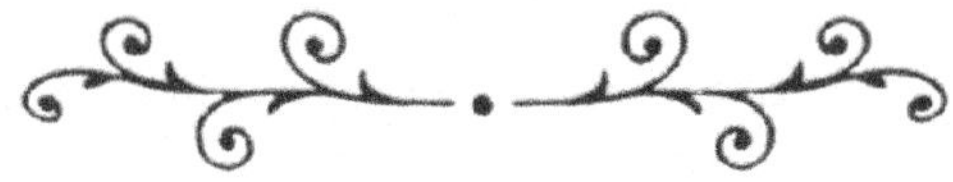

"You sure you're okay with this?" Cole asked.

Aria leaned her elbows on the rickety fence, looking out on the overgrown pasture of the ranch she'd grown up on as she stood beside her brother.

"You're right. It has to happen sooner or later," Aria declared. "Renting it out hasn't been good for the ranch. It's fallen into disrepair. And if you need the money, then it's for the best."

"I know Allister would probably be able to let me buy in over time, or I could borrow against this place…" Cole let the sentence trail off, but Aria knew this wasn't an ideal situation for Cole.

"No. You're right. It's time." When Cole told her about his plans, it was as if she received the final push she needed to move on.

They stood side by side, as if reliving past events they both struggled with. Hers were more recent.

But this was their home, the place they had both grown up.

"And you're okay with selling it to Lucas?" Cole asked.

Aria held the question for a moment, giving it some space.

"Who better to buy it than the one man who sincerely admired our dad?" she reasoned, with a sigh of resignation. Her eyes drifted over the pasture to the small barn Lucas and their father had built together. Lucas had hinted to Aria that, if things went the way he hoped, they could maybe get married in it.

Her father was intensely proud of the barn and the work Lucas had put into it, often pointing out to Aria that Lucas was handier than Cole.

At that time, Aria was deeply in love with Lucas and felt proud of the fact that her boyfriend was so capable.

That her father liked him.

"Maybe," Cole agreed. "They sure had some kind of relationship."

Aria heard the yearning note in Cole's voice. "You sound a little melancholy."

Cole waved off her question, looking over at her, his expression serious. "You know better than that."

Aria held his narrowed eyes, knowing what he referred to.

And yet…

She was about to say more when the sound of a diesel engine broke into the moment. A truck drove past the house and pulled up in front of the small barn.

Lucas got out of the truck, but he was alone this time.

His cowboy hat shaded his features. His plain twill shirt was rolled up over muscular forearms and tucked into faded blue jeans. The large silver buckle on his belt glinted in the sun as he walked toward them, his long lean legs eating up the distance.

He was only an inch taller than Cole, but the hat and the way he carried himself made him look more than that.

He pulled off his sunglasses and tucked them into his pocket, and his eyes immediately found Aria's.

She wanted to look away but realized that would only make him realize what effect he had on her. So, instead, she held his steady gaze and lifted her chin just enough to challenge him.

"Hey, there," he said, his deep voice quiet. Lucas never had to speak up. Just his very presence made people pay attention. "Glad we could meet at the ranch."

He pulled his gaze away from Aria, looking around the yard, smiling. "Lots of wonderful memories here, that's for sure."

Beyond the barn was the arena where, Aria knew, many of those very memories were made.

"I'll always appreciate the time your father spent with me," Lucas said. "He was definitely a man to admire."

Neither Cole nor Aria said anything, letting Lucas' comments drift away on the faint breeze teasing Aria's hair.

Lucas leaned on the fence as well, pulling back, however, when the rail beneath his arms cracked and almost gave way.

"Guess that will need fixing."

"That and a few other things. Our previous renter wasn't much for maintenance." Cole straightened, shoving his hands into the back pockets of his jeans. "Did you want to walk around the place? See what you think?"

Lucas shot him a puzzled look. "You're not having second thoughts, are you?"

"No. Just thinking you might change your mind once you see the place up close. It's been a few years."

"And you're on board with this?" Lucas asked Aria.

"I am," she said, avoiding his gaze this time. "It's time to move on."

Lucas thankfully said nothing to that.

"Where do you want to start?" Cole asked.

"We could start right here. If you have the time, that is."

Grady shot a sidelong glance at Aria, raising his eyebrows at her, as if giving her a chance to leave.

She gave him a careful smile, thankful for the reprieve,

and was about to make her excuses when Cole's cell phone rang.

He pulled it out of his shirt pocket, looking down at the screen. "I have to take this. I'll be right back."

He walked away from them, swiping across the screen, then talking to the person on the other end of the line, his voice lowered.

Lucas watched him leave, then turned to Aria, his hands strung up in the pockets of his blue jeans. "This might not necessarily be an appropriate thing to say, but I'm thankful you're willing to sell me and Burke this place. It's a great opportunity for me, and it means a lot to be able to work on the place where I had some of my greatest experiences."

Aria's heart jolted at his words, but as she glanced at him, she saw him looking toward the arena.

Foolish girl, she told herself. *He's talking about his time spent with my father.*

Not her.

She wished Cole would finish up so she could leave, but just as she formulated that thought, her brother returned, looking apologetic.

"Sorry, I've got to leave. Joe Brewer has a horse with pregnancy complications. It's one of his pure-bred mares." He glanced over at Lucas. "I imagine it's okay if Aria shows you around?"

Lucas nodded, but Aria sensed he would have preferred to be with Cole.

Was it that hard to be around her?

That's when her pride and Waldren tenacity kicked in. "I probably know more about the place than you do anyway," she contended, sending a wry look toward her brother.

"Won't dispute that. You went riding on the ranch way more than I ever did." He gave a nod to Lucas. "I'm sure we'll be in touch." Then he left.

Silence followed in his wake, and Aria wasn't sure how to

break it. She tugged her cardigan closer around her, as if protecting herself with the flimsy barrier.

"May as well start with the pasture," she said, walking toward the gate, which hung open, supported by a single rusty hinge. She tried not to feel embarrassed at the state of the ranch. She had been gone for four years before her father died, and neither she nor Cole, when he came back to Aspen Valley, were interested in running it. As a result, it had been rented for almost ten years now.

"So, who was your last renter?"

"Paul Gelke, brother of Bill, the real estate agent."

"I'm surprised you rented it to him."

His words were innocent enough, but his tone held a note of condemnation. Or at least that's how she read it.

"He was buddies with my dad."

"Really? I'm surprised. Paul wasn't the straightest shooter." His bewilderment showed her there were parts of her father he had probably not been privy to.

"No. More of a scattershot character." Aria had never approved of Paul, and after her father died, she had hoped to rent the land to Kip Cosgrove or the Bannisters. "He finagled a ten-year lease out of my dad. That ran out last fall, thank goodness, so we would either have to find another renter or sell it."

"Like I said, I'm thankful for the opportunity."

He made it sound like they had approached him, rather than the other way around.

No matter, it was time to sell.

"So, like we said, it hasn't been well cared for. Paul didn't rent by the acre or by how many head of cattle he ran. It was a flat fee that he and my father negotiated."

The grass they walked through was a thick mat, and Aria had to be careful how she stepped. Thankfully, she had worn flats to work today rather than her usual high heels.

"Looks like I'll need to run harrows over this a bunch of times," Lucas commented.

"Will you be getting cows on it right away?"

"Not for a couple of months. We want to look around. Look for a herd dispersal."

"In that case, you would want to mow it first. The grass is high in places. You could get some hay out of the process."

"That's a really good idea. Thanks."

And why did his simple comment warm her heart so much?

Because you've spent too much time looking for affirmation in the wrong places?

"The rest of the pasture is much the same. Don't know how far you want to walk."

"I might come by with one of the horses tomorrow, if that's okay. Check out the back fields."

"We've got a quad you can use."

"Nah. I prefer to ride my horse. Get some real riding in instead of that bronc riding I've been doing way too long."

Part of her wanted to ask about his rodeo days, but why? It would only bring back the memories crowding at the edge of her mind.

Best to keep things arm's length.

"Can we check out the arena?" he asked.

Aria just nodded, trying not to look at her watch. To fidget with the sleeves of her cardigan. This was probably good for her. Hopefully, being around him would condition her to his presence. Keep those stupid emotions that she thought she had conquered at bay.

The door to the arena also hung askew. As they stepped inside, she turned on the lights and saw a flash of white and grey streak across the dirt and disappear behind the boards circling the arena area.

"What was that?" Lucas asked.

"One of the many feral cats we've got roaming around

here. Paul was always going to catch them, but he never could."

"Descendants of Pixie?" he asked.

His voice held a joshing note she envied. She wished she could be as casual around him as he seemed to be around her. Time would make that happen, she promised herself. Time and exposure.

"Probably."

"She was the most personable cat I've ever met."

"You certainly played with her enough."

"I was always surprised your dad let you have her in the house. He hated cats, didn't he?"

"He didn't like pets, period. Claimed they were an unnecessary expense."

"As if horses are cheap to feed," he joked.

Aria wasn't sure what to say to that, surprised at his comment. Instead, she walked ahead of him to the fence surrounding the arena floor. Despite the darkness, weeds poked their way through the dirt and sawdust.

Lucas shook the fence around the arena, nodding his approval. "This is at least solid, and it looks like the roof it still good, despite the cobwebs and dust."

"When dad built this place, he said he built it to last."

Lucas walked onto the dirt of the arena, hands in his pockets, and despite her desire to keep him at arm's length, she couldn't help watching as he looked around, smiling.

A few of the memories that she'd shoved way back slowly encroached. Times she would be practicing with Courtney and Desni, racing their horses around the barrels, dust flying up from the horse's hooves, music blaring from the speakers she'd talked her father into installing.

Times she would be sitting on the small set of bleachers her father had built at one end of the arena, watching Lucas and Cole practice roping. They had visions of competing as a team, but Cole had struggled. Didn't help that their father was always critical of Cole's efforts.

Somehow, Lucas had managed to find his way into her father's confidence. They were interested in the same things, and Lucas exhibited an inherent ability to ride wild, rank horses.

"I learned so much here," he reminisced. "Lessons that helped me get to where I did bronc riding. Couldn't have done what I did, gotten to where I have, without his guidance and encouragement."

While she wondered what made him quit, she knew not to involve herself in his life.

"In your mind, the arena hasn't lost any value?" she asked, keeping things on a practical level.

"Not at all. It needs some work, but it won't take much to bring it back to its former glory." He leaned on a fence, smiling. "I'll always be thankful for the skills your father taught me. We made many good memories here." He looked at Aria, as if expecting her to join in on the reminiscing.

But she didn't reply. Sure, she had some good times in this arena. Some fun.

But since coming back, there were other, darker events embedded in this ranch.

Difficult memories she struggled to reconcile.

"Let's go look at the rest of the place," was all she said.

She spun around and walked out into the light, hoping to leave the darkness behind.

"LISTEN UP, everyone. This is the scene where the extras come on." Courtney motioned to Lucas and Kip Cosgrove. "In the original novel, this is the ball scene, but we're turning it into a square dance."

"What about the boot scooting boogie?" Lucas brushed

the sawdust off his shirt and walked over to the group gathered for this scene.

He hadn't been too keen on joining the play as an extra, but when Kip said he would, Lucas couldn't let him have one over on him. He and Kip's paths had crossed at various rodeos, and it was always a good time when they got together.

"Do you still know how to do-si-do?" Kip asked, as he and Lucas joined the group.

"Hey. I can Allemande Left with the best of them."

"This I'd love to see."

Grady and Aria stood off to one side, chatting. Aria laughed at something Grady said and Lucas tried not to feel jealous of their interaction. Through the Aspen Valley grapevine, he'd heard that they had dated when she had come back. He wondered how Grady had let someone like Aria slip through his fingers.

Like you did?

The words accused even as they created a low-level discomfort.

I had my reasons, he reminded himself. And at the time, they were valid.

"We're running through this a bunch of times," Courtney announced. "I've got Dennis Elzinga, our ever-helpful town counsellor, to teach us the basic dance steps. We're not getting real fancy because we'll need space for Mr. Darcy and Miss Bennet to speak their lines."

"We keep this play going long enough, Grady is going to forget his name," Kip muttered.

"As long as he doesn't think he's the richest and most eligible man in Aspen Valley," Lucas returned with a chuckle.

"I don't know. He's pretty eligible, and women seem to think he's easy on the eyes. I know Nicole was asking me why he's not married."

"Things so boring at your place that you're gossiping with your wife?" Lucas teased.

Kip just grinned and shrugged, turning his attention back to Courtney, who was pairing people up.

Lucas ended up with Brooke, whom Courtney had somehow roped into helping, and Kip was paired with his wife. Lucky him.

"So, I guess we're going to be dancing together," Lucas said to Brooke, grinning down at her.

"Just help me out, okay?" Brooke asked, releasing a heavy sigh. "I have two left feet. This was not my vision when I signed up for this play."

"Well, we should be okay then," Lucas returned. "I have two right feet."

Brooke chuckled at that, and just for fun, Lucas gave her a quick hug. He looked around, surprised to see Grady staring at him, frowning.

What was that about?

"You guys know the whole square dance routine. Dennis will call out the steps, and I'll be helping Grady and Aria with their lines." She glanced over at the short, squat man beside her wearing an oversize cowboy hat, handlebar mustache, plaid shirt, and a buckle bigger than any Lucas had ever seen any rodeo cowboy wear.

"Wonder where he got that hardware," Lucas whispered to Brooke. "The dollar store?"

Courtney fired him a warning look, and Lucas just shrugged.

"I want everyone to stand beside their partners," Dennis called out. "Men on the left, women on the right, and stand in a square. Remember where you are. This is called Home for each couple. We'll start with a basic move called circle to the left and then circle to the right."

They all clasped hands, getting ready to follow his instructions. Lucas and Brooke stood, holding hands, facing Aria and Grady.

Again, Lucas caught Grady watching him, mistrust flitting over his features.

Aria wasn't even looking at him.

Dennis worked them through a few steps, which they repeated until they got them right, then Courtney stepped in again.

"You'll be doing some basic moves that we'll be adjusting to work with the dialogue," Courtney put in. "This is where Mr. Darcy and Miss Bennet will have the conversation that shows up on page eighteen. Got it?"

Aria and Grady nodded.

"And we'll be moving slowly through this all, okay? To give everyone time to speak, and so the audience can hear what they say." Courtney turned to Dennis. "I think it best if the couple opposite Aria and Grady come forward, move past them and then come back. Like a Do Si Do with couples."

"Sure thing."

"You guys got this?"

Everyone nodded, and they squared up again. They ran through a few more steps as Courtney explained what they would say when.

The caller issued their instructions and the beat, and Aria spoke her lines. Grady replied, his tone wooden, which, at this point in the story, suited the moment. Mr. Darcy was awkward in this scene. But as the scene progressed, Grady missed lines, blushing every time he and Brooke had to move around each other. He was supposed to be fascinated by Elizabeth Bennet, but Lucas could see that Grady only had eyes for Brooke.

Lucas stifled a smile, and one moment when he and Brooke were supposed to move forward and touch hands with Aria and Grady, he caught Aria's eye and winked at her.

She suppressed her own smile as Grady botched his lines again. Everyone groaned as they had to start over.

This time, when Grady hesitated, Lucas prompted him. The second time Grady did it, Lucas helped him out again.

"Looks like you know my lines better than I do," Grady muttered with an embarrassed chuckle.

Lucas suspected it was Brooke's presence that confused Grady. He was tempted to tell him to just ask her out already.

They finished the supposed dance, and each time Grady muffed his lines even worse. It was only thanks to Lucas' prompting that he got through the scene.

Courtney didn't look too pleased with how things were going. Lucas didn't blame her. They were on a tight production schedule. When she pulled Grady aside, Lucas wasn't surprised.

The other cast members went back to whatever they were doing before being summoned for the scene.

But Aria was frowning at Grady and Courtney, and Lucas wasn't too eager to leave, so he lingered.

"What do you think they're talking about?"

Aria blew out a sigh. "Grady's been having more and more trouble with his lines. I think he's distracted." She looked around the room, then lowered her voice. "I think it's Brooke that's causing it."

"Oh, you noticed too."

Aria tugged on the sleeves of her cardigan. "I wish Brooke would notice."

"She still stuck on George?"

"I think so. Though she hasn't been eating at the Grill and Chill that much anymore. So, here's hoping."

"Well, the heart wants what the heart wants."

Aria shot him a puzzled look. "That sounds almost profound."

"You have that 'coming from you' tone in your voice." He didn't want her surprise to bother him, but it did. "Yes. Lucas read books."

"I didn't mean it that way," she said as her cheeks flushed. "I just meant-"

"It's okay." He held up his hand to stop anything else she

might say. They were veering into territory he didn't want to explore while they both stood in the middle of Aspen Valley Hall with more than a dozen people milling around. "I better get back to set-making. Don't want Burke to nag me about working on his own. Brothers, know what I mean?" He kept his tone light and sauntered off, resisting the urge to look behind to see if she was watching him.

Chapter 5

"You're absolutely sure about this?" Lucas took the papers Aria had just put together and glanced at them, his elbows resting on her desk.

He had laid his cowboy hat beside him, his bare head giving him a curiously vulnerable look. His hair, thick as ever, shone in the overhead lights, and his head now bent over the document.

"Yes. Cole and I talked about it some more last night, after the rehearsal. We need to…to move on."

To her dismay, her voice had the tiniest catch, which she hoped Lucas wouldn't notice. It bothered her that selling the ranch affected her emotions. She should be glad to put the place behind her and move on.

But still…

"Though I'm sure it can't be easy for you, I want to say that I appreciate that you're willing to sell." Lucas looked up and gave her a careful smile. "I know you could have sold it to just anybody. It means a lot to me to work a ranch and farm that held such wonderful memories for me."

Aria presumed he was talking about working with her father.

Then he looked up, and his eyes held hers, and she wondered if he was including their past relationship in his comment.

She couldn't look away and, unfortunately, didn't want to.

Had he thought of her much after he left? Because she often thought about him.

Awkwardness floated around her like a cloud, and she wished she could treat him like any other man she ran across in Aspen Valley. Treat him like she treated Quinn DeVries, who was better looking than Lucas but was simply an acquaintance. Treat him like Grady Thomas, who was more settled, kinder, and an all-around good person.

But she and Lucas had a deeper, more intimate history than all the other single men in Aspen Valley.

Weariness clawed at her as she tired of the questions that hovered and clung. He wasn't leaving. Neither was she. May as well bring everything out into the open and get it out of the way.

"What made you come back to Aspen Valley?" she asked, choosing to start with an easy one. Sort of.

She knew he hadn't come back for her.

Lucas tapped his pen on the papers, then looked up.

"Interesting that you ask me that," he returned, not really answering her question. "You're the one that always wanted to leave. I was the one that wanted to stay."

"I did leave to go to school."

Her desire to get a law degree was one thing that had created a distance between them. He had hoped she would find a local job. Settle into Aspen Valley. But she had other dreams.

And their relationship grew strained. Then, just when she realized she missed him more than she wanted a law degree and considered about coming back, he broke up with her. Told her he was leaving Aspen Valley for good.

"And now you're back too," he finished.

"Yes. I guess I missed my friends and my community."

"So, here we are. You wanted to leave and came back. I wanted to stay and came back."

"Aspen Valley seems to have that pull."

"It does. So does family. To answer your question, that was one of the other reasons I came back. I got tired of not having a home. A place to come back to at the end of the rodeo season. Tired of the stress and the younger guys chasing after my buckles and trophies." Then he shrugged, glancing down at the papers he had just signed.

Papers which would change a lot for him, Aria thought.

He continued, "And it didn't help that my hips and knees were letting me know I couldn't put them through all that bucking and spurring, never mind getting bucked off, anymore. I had to admit, riding broncs is a young man's game."

He looked back at her, giving her a hint of the crooked smile that used to make her knees weak.

"You're not that old," she couldn't help saying.

"Thanks for that. According to some of the youngsters at the last rodeo I was at, I was an old-timer. Practically a pioneer. Sort of how I viewed your dad whenever we worked together."

Aria just nodded, knowing that any conversation with Lucas would, invariably, include mention of her father.

"But I sure felt my age the last time I got bucked off and landed wrong. Took me way too long to get up and to get mobile again." A wistful look crossed his face, and Aria sensed that no matter his reasons for coming back, rodeo and riding saddle broncs would always be a part of his life.

Her father had been the same.

"Injuries have a way of reminding you that there's only so much you can do to your body before it rebels," she returned.

Lucas tilted his head to one side, as if remembering. "Like that time you broke your arm trying to swing from the barn rafters? You were in a cast for what seemed like months. And I know it bothered you for years after."

"Still does." She clenched and unclenched her fist. One of the exercises Patrice had given her to do when Aria visited her about a wrist, permanently weakened because of that very break.

"And what about your hip? Is that better?"

Another casual reference to a shared moment. A horse had bucked her off while she and Lucas were out riding. Thankfully, they hadn't been far from the ranch when it happened.

"Yeah. That doesn't bother me anymore."

"I remember being terrified when I saw you fly off. I thought for sure you were going to die."

"Is that why you were so angry with me?" she couldn't help asking.

"I wasn't angry. Just so scared and worried. I know it didn't come out that way." His smile deepened enough to bring out a dimple in one cheek. She wished her heart didn't give that unwelcome flip of attraction. Surely, after all this time, she should be done with him.

Shouldn't she?

"Despite the injuries, we had some good times, didn't we?" he asked, his smile still in place.

Again, that spark of connection she thought was long extinguished.

But right behind that came a surge of frustrated anger. How dare he just come back, so casually, treating a relationship that had been her anchor like it was some adorable little high school fling.

"We had some, and then we didn't anymore," was all she managed.

"I'm…I'm sorry for that."

Sorry. Such a small word to cover all the heartache she felt. The pain and feeling of abandonment.

She pushed herself away from her desk and stood. "Thanks for coming in to sign the papers. I'll send everything off to Land Titles and then wait while it winds through their endless process. I'll let you know what I need from you next."

Lucas was slower to stand, and by the puzzled look on his face, Aria guessed the conversation hadn't gone the way he hoped.

It hadn't gone the way she hoped, either.

She thought they could shift into a different space. Thought she could banter with him like they used to.

But the way his smile crept into her soul, niggling at shared memories, showed her the foolishness of that notion, at least for now.

The memories they shared were strong reminders to keep her distance from him, as much as that was possible in a town like Aspen Valley. In time, the casualness would come. In time, she would find someone she could care about and who would care enough for her to make sacrifices for her.

Unlike Lucas, who always put his own dreams first.

He shoved his hat back on his head and reverted so quickly back to the old Lucas that it made her heart spin.

"Thanks again for all this." Lucas gestured to the papers still laying on the desk. "It means so much to me. Your father was very important to me."

"I know he was." And that was the closest she was getting to the memories she knew he wanted to share with her.

Besides their broken relationship, one of the last things she wanted to talk about was her father.

Lucas hesitated a moment, then with a quick nod, he turned and left.

She watched him go, her arms crossed tightly across her midsection, pulling in a slow breath.

Too easily, she remembered their last conversation before he left. He had told her how he had always wanted to ride rodeo and be the best saddle bronc rider in North America. Maybe even match her father's winnings.

He couldn't do that and date her as well.

He couldn't make that sacrifice for her.

Maybe she'd been selfish in hoping he would. Just after graduation, he had professed his undying love for her. Told her he wanted to settle down with her.

With a shake of her head, she dismissed the memories as the meanderings of a foolish heart. She had put too much stock in the words of a twenty-one-year-old boy.

A boy she had dated since she was fifteen and had a crush on since she was twelve. Someone she thought would take her away from Aspen Valley.

And her father.

"I JUST WANT to make sure you're okay with all of this." Cole held the purchase agreement in his hand, glancing over it at Aria.

She curled her feet up in her favorite chair in her apartment, taking another sip of her glass of wine. "Why are you asking now? Lucas has already signed the documents."

"I know. Just want to make sure that you're okay with Lucas buying it."

"May as well be him as anyone else." Aria let the wine burn its way down her throat, easing away the tension she'd felt all day after Lucas had left the office. "He was more invested in that place than either you or I were. Probably spent more time there, matter of fact."

"Not if you count all the grunt work we did putting up fences."

"It made us who we are," she said, raising her glass in a quick toast, her voice taking on a harsh note.

"Fine upstanding citizens," Cole returned, the same tone in his voice.

He bent over and scrawled his signature on the line Aria had marked with a sticky note, then pushed the papers back at her. He leaned back in the couch, resting his one leg over his knee, his hands wrapped behind his head.

"End of an era," he said with a heavy sigh. "I wish I felt happier about it."

"Please don't tell me you're changing your mind after all the paperwork and second guessing I've done," Aria pleaded.

"No. Not at all." He waved off her concern. "I just thought that knowing I'll be able to buy out Allister would make me feel…well…more excited."

"It's a great opportunity, and the money we get from the ranch will give you more than enough to buy him out and build your house."

"Just think how much it could have been if our dear father hadn't sold off so much of the place." His voice was hard, unyielding as the mountains they looked over.

"Thankfully, he didn't live long enough to do that." As soon as she spoke the words, she felt a shiver of guilt. "I shouldn't have said that."

"Don't worry. I've thought the same. Wasn't easy living on that place with dad and his horrible temper."

"I'm glad you got away."

"And you should have stayed away." Then Cole lifted his hand in a gesture of apology. "Sorry. I shouldn't spout off."

"No. You're right. I should have. But when I was in school, I missed Lucas, so I came back. It was a mistake, that's for sure." She rubbed her forehead with her hand, wishing she could erase the memories. She didn't want her past to define her and yet, it very much colored who she was now.

"I always thought he was the way he was because he hated me so much."

"I don't know if he hated you," Aria said, her voice quiet. "He got worse after Mom died, though."

"Talking to Doris made me realize that anger is part of grieving, but it still puzzled me why he took it out on me."

"We'll never know." Aria stretched her legs out and rested them on the low table between them as she slouched down into the couch. She took the last sip of wine and set the empty goblet on the end table beside her, pressing her lips together as she puzzled out her next comment.

"So, enough about the past. Let's talk about the future. How is Courtney feeling? She seemed pale at the last rehearsal."

"The last week she's been throwing up most every morning. So much that even Fenna has learned to come running with an empty pail when Courtney wakes up."

"That's an interesting life skill for an eight-year-old to know. Do you think she'll want to carry on with the play?"

" Don't even bring that question up around her. I tried to ask her if she should ease off, and I got an earful."

"She's pretty devoted to this play."

"Tell me about it." Cole shrugged. "But she's happy, and, despite seeing my wife so ill, that makes me happy. I just hope that things will continue to go well. After the baby is born."

Aria sensed a note of reservation in his voice and instinctively knew what he was referring to.

"You don't have to worry. You'll make a wonderful father. I see how you are with Fenna, so I'm not concerned."

He offered her a tight smile. "Thanks for the affirmation."

"You're not our father." Aria's voice held a fierce note of determination. "You're so not like him."

Cole just nodded, and Aria knew she couldn't do anything more than continue to assure him as, she was sure, Courtney did as well.

Then her phone rang, and she glanced down, frowning.

"It's Courtney," she said, swiping quickly over the screen. "Hey, girl. How's things?"

"Great. Just great."

But she didn't sound like they were great.

"What's wrong?"

"Nothing. Just tell Cole not to leave his phone behind. If he's still there."

"He is." She covered her phone. "Your wife said not to leave your phone at home."

Cole's eyes widened as he patted his pockets. "I can't believe I did that. Everything's okay."

"I heard," Courtney returned. "Ask him if he can stop at the grocery store on his way back and get some eggs and bread."

Aria relayed the message as Cole nodded.

Then a pause.

"Is that all you wanted?"

A deep sigh told Aria that it wasn't.

"I didn't want to bug you," Courtney continued, "but now that I have you…I just got a call from Grady, our leading man. His mother is very sick, and he's going down to see her. He's not sure how long he'll be gone."

"So, you just get someone to take his place for a while. They only need to be able to read lines back to me until he can come back."

"That's what I thought, too. I've been on the phone all day trying to find a replacement. No go. I was wondering if you had any ideas."

"If worse comes to worse, we could get a girl to stand in," Aria suggested. "Or Cole."

He waved his hands wildly, eyes wide as he shook his head.

Guess that was a no.

"I thought the same, but if things go really bad with Grady's mom, and he can't come back…."

Oh boy. This play was going off the rails. Poor Courtney. No wonder she sounded so stressed.

"I see where you're going. We might need a replacement. Well, rehearsal isn't until the day after tomorrow. I'll see what I can come up with."

"I'll keep trying, too, but I thought I should let you know."

"Thanks."

Aria said goodbye and dropped her phone onto the couch beside her, shaking her head at her brother.

"Chicken."

"Realist. There's no way I'm speaking those lines to my sister."

Aria chuckled at the horror on his face.

"I can see that. And Courtney wants you to pick up some eggs and bread on your way out."

"Not milk? It's usually milk. Fenna and Courtney drink gallons of it."

"If you're still eating cold cereal, the way you used to, I'm sure you're as much to blame as they are."

"Nah. Courtney is trying to break me of the habit."

"Still a Honey-Nut Cheerios fan?"

"It's the only kind."

"I remember sneaking boxes of it into the house."

"Never had to when Mom was around."

They both grew quiet, serious.

"Are you doing what I'm doing?" Aria asked.

"Probably." Cole dragged his hands over his face, but then gave Aria a smile. "Each month helps me move further from the memories. And seeing a counsellor has been good for me, too." He held her eyes a second longer than necessary.

"Dad never..." his sentence trailed off, holding an unspoken question.

"I know where you're going, but no. Never. Even he had some standards," she said, unable to stifle her harsh tone.

Cole seemed to sag with relief. "I used to wonder. I know he seemed to dote on you. Spoil you even."

"Seemed being the operative word." Aria could not keep the bitterness out of her voice. "Trust me, I would far sooner have received a loving or kind word from him than all the gifts and trips he gave me."

Cole was quiet a moment, then stood and walked over. He dropped down beside her and gave her a loving hug. "You know I pray for you every day."

"I'm glad you do," she said, her arms wrapped around him, her head lying on his shoulder. "I have a hard time talking to God. Thinking of him as a father."

"It took me some time, too." Her brother pulled away, resting his hand on her shoulder. "But Courtney and I found our way through it all together. And talking to Doris has really helped. Think about it."

Aria just shrugged. "I will. Though I feel like it's all in the past now. Why dig it up?"

"Because dad's been gone only four years."

"And I haven't been around Aspen Valley for longer than that." She gave him a good-natured smile. "I'm getting past it. I don't want this to define me. I'm stronger than that."

"What about Lucas?"

She shot her brother a tight frown. "What about him?"

"Are you stronger than your old relationship with him?"

She heard a faint warning note in his voice that created a shiver of apprehension.

"He walked away from me, remember? And that was many years ago as well. Time heals a lot of wounds."

"I know. But I also know that the scars those wounds leave can take longer to forget."

Aria just shrugged. "Don't concern yourself with me and Lucas. Fool me once…"

"You sound pretty tough, but despite how long ago it was, I know you were as hurt as Courtney was when I left."

His words teased out another thought.

"Do you think there was another reason Lucas left? Something he doesn't want to tell me? Just like with you and Courtney?"

The look Cole gave her was a combination of sympathy, which annoyed her, mingled with veiled frustration, which annoyed her even more.

"Lucas admired Dad so much that everything he did was for him. Because of him."

"So, he chose Dad over me, is what you're saying?" Aria tried to inject a teasing tone into her voice but couldn't quite hit it.

"I'm saying that he had other priorities. And Dad was very much mixed in with that."

Cole's words held a ring of truth. Then the previous thought that had risen, now hovered, as if waiting to be given more time and attention.

"Anyhow, I would just be careful around Lucas."

"Don't worry. I will. I can't go through that again."

Cole gave her a gentle smile, then he walked out of the apartment.

But as he closed the door, he left behind a swirl of confusion. She knew Cole hadn't liked Lucas much, even before he broke her heart.

That was enough reason to stay away from the guy.

Chapter 6

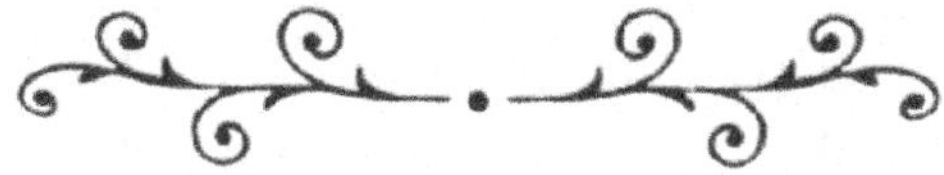

Lucas heaved the piece of plywood his brother had just cut across the hall to the stage, where it would be supported and painted.

"Things are coming along at a good pace," Burke said as he set it against the supports Klint had just hammered together. "This is the last background we have to paint."

"And then what?"

"Set design and costumes," Karissa put in, bringing a couple of cans of paint onto the plastic-covered stage.

"What do I get to wear?" Lucas asked.

"You'll have to raid your closet for a plaid shirt and blue jeans," his sister-in-law returned.

"What? I don't get a waistcoat?" Lucas brushed the sawdust off his current pair of blue jeans. "I thought the book was set in the Regency era."

"That you even know that tidbit of information speaks well to that brain I know you haven't used much," Burke teased, joining them.

"I is educated," Lucas returned, putting his hand on his heart in mock dismay.

"You may be educated, but you're not picking up on the

vibe here," Burke said, putting a table down in front of one of the already completed backgrounds. "Read the room, buddy. This is Pride and Prejudice in the West."

"Wow. I didn't know that," Lucas returned, sarcasm edging his voice. "But I thought we could dial up the glamor."

"Well, dial it down." Courtney joined them, looking around with a critical eye. "We're trying to keep expenses down and hassle down and stress levels down."

"You sound like your stress level hasn't seen 'down' for a few months," Lucas couldn't help teasing her.

"It's fine." Then she glanced over the group. "What I need to help with the stress levels is to have a volunteer to read for Grady's part. Male. Female. Doesn't matter."

"Did Grady duck out?" Kip called out from the back of the room, where he was cutting up some lumber.

"No, thank goodness, but he's still with his mother, who hasn't improved much. I'm not sure how long he'll be gone, and I need someone to stand in for him until he can come back."

And for some unfathomable reason, Courtney's eyes landed on Lucas.

Lucas held his hand up. "No. I'm not doing that." The last thing he wanted was to pretend to be in love with a woman he was still half in love with. A woman who had always haunted his thoughts.

A woman he didn't deserve.

"It's just until Grady gets back. And I've watched you. You know his lines better than he does."

"I'm a natural born mimic," Lucas said with a shrug.

"Perfect. You can mimic being Mr. Darcy, owner of one of the largest ranches in Dorchester County."

And before he could protest again, she strode away.

Lucas watched her leave, feeling like his mouth was hanging open in shock. He turned to his brother. "So, did that just happen?"

"Looks like it, Mr. Darcy."

Lucas wanted to smack the smug look off his brother's face.

"Well, at least it's just until Grady comes back."

"What if he doesn't?" Karissa joined Burke, slipping her arm around her husband's waist. "What if you're stuck in the role?"

"He'll come back. I know he will." But Lucas felt like he was trying to convince himself more than anyone else.

He was about to go after Courtney to tell her he wasn't going to do it when Aria entered the hall, and he saw Courtney walk up to her. They talked, their voices muffled by the noise in the hall, and then he saw Aria shoot a panicked glance his way. She turned back to Courtney, and it looked like she was protesting. Vehemently.

Her apparent anger was like a prod. Why should it matter so much to her that he was a temp for Grady? Should it be that big a deal?

He knew he wasn't her favorite person, but surely after all this time she should have gotten over it. Shouldn't she?

At any rate, the way she was frowning and motioning with her hands tipped him into irritation territory.

So, he sauntered over, exaggerating the rolling gait some of his rodeo buddies perfected. He wished he had his cowboy hat on so he could push it to the back of his head, enhancing the pose.

He had to make do with stopping in front of them both, standing hipshot, his thumbs strung up in the loops of his blue jeans, one side of his mouth curved into a mocking grin.

"So, Elizabeth, guess you're stuck with a new Mr. Darcy for the next while."

Aria's gaze flicked over him, then back to Courtney, tilting her head, silently communicating her disapproval.

"I'm glad you agreed to help out," was all Courtney said, and she strode away before Aria could say anything more.

She pulled in a few quick breaths, then turned to him, all smiles.

But he knew Aria well enough to see that she was simply drawing on her innate acting ability.

"Thanks for helping out," she offered.

"Just doing my part for the greater good."

"Okay then, let's run some lines before rehearsal."

Lucas was about to say he didn't have a script when Courtney returned and slapped one into his hands, then left, calling out directions to the rest of the cast.

"She seems to be kind of stressed," Lucas couldn't help saying.

"She's had to replace a leading lady and a leading man. She's tired and pregnant, so I guess that's to be expected." Then Aria shot him a horrified look, clapping her hand over her mouth.

"I'm guessing from your reaction, I'm not supposed to know."

Then, to his surprise, Aria put her hand on his shoulder, giving him a light shake. "No one is supposed to know. It slipped out."

He mimed locking his lips and throwing away the key, something they used to do when they were playing in the fort that Courtney, Aria, and Cole had built in Courtney's yard.

Aria must have remembered as well, as her smile veered from forced to more natural.

"Glad to know you remember the old protocol."

"You pounded it into me. I don't know how many of your secrets I kept over the years. And those were only the ones I knew about." His comment was innocent, but it hinted at other things he knew Aria kept from him.

Her expression grew somber, as if she was remembering some of those very things.

"You okay?" he asked.

She looked dazed for a moment, then pulled in another quick breath.

"Yeah. Fine."

He held up his script. "I guess we should get to this," he said with a quick smile, not wanting to delve too deeply into the past.

"Right."

"This is the scene where Mr. Darcy gives Elizabeth the letter he wrote defending himself."

"Yes."

"Does this guy have a first name?" he asked, looking down at the script. It's Mr. Darcy this and Darcy that."

"I believe it's Fitzwilliam."

Lucas groaned. "No wonder he wants to stick with Darcy." He glanced at the lines. "Okay, from the top of page thirty-one."

He cleared his throat and began.

"Miz Bennet, I been a walkin' around this here pasture, waitin' for you."

Aria glanced down at her script, then up at Lucas. "That's not what is says."

"Well, I thought I would countrify it. This is Pride and Prejudice western version."

"No one out here talks like that."

"Not yet."

She chuckled, and he felt the tension that had hummed between them ease a bit.

"I'd like for you to read this letter," Lucas continued, then pretended to hand it to her. Then he frowned, reading the rest of the script. "So, then he just turns and walks away?"

"Yes. Elizabeth is dumbfounded to see him here."

"Sort of like you looked when you found out you had to work with me," he teased. May as well act normal, which, he figured, was the quickest way to get to feeling normal.

"Then I read the letter out loud," Aria said, "and add my own thoughts as I do."

"Censoring as you go?"

"I guess."

"But doesn't what he says touch you deeply?" Lucas tried for a woebegone look.

"Not really. He is rather critical and presumptuous."

"Well, he's Fitzwilliam Darcy. He owns a lot of land and is a real catch. I guess he can do some presumpting now and then."

This elicited a light chuckle, which made him feel even more relaxed.

"So now you're gone, and the next scene is with my sisters."

"Ah yes, the flighty and inconsiderate siblings."

Another laugh.

This might work out okay after all, he thought. *We can find a way to be casual around each other.*

But then she looked up at him, their eyes met, their gazes melded, and he felt as if everything around him fell away.

His breath caught in his throat, and he had to clench his hands to keep from reaching up and touching her cheek.

Like he used to.

"Okay. We're shifting back a few scenes," Courtney called out. "We're re-doing the dance scene. Just in case."

"In case of what?" Brooke called out.

"In case of any more disasters raining down on this production."

"There's more disasters?" Lucas asked.

Courtney gave him a pointed gaze, then shook her head as if she was done talking.

"I should talk to her after." Lucas shook his head, rolling and unrolling the script in his hands.

"And do what?"

"Offer her some support? I'm not sure. She needs some encouragement for this play to keep going."

Aria said nothing, and he shot her a sidelong look. Once again, it seemed neither could look away, but he caught a hint of pain in the depths of her eyes.

He wondered what caused it, hoped it wasn't him.

Then he dismissed the thought. After he had left Aspen Valley, he found out that Aria hadn't wasted much time and had started dating again. Obviously, the heart he thought he had broken had recuperated quickly.

His had taken much longer.

Chapter 7

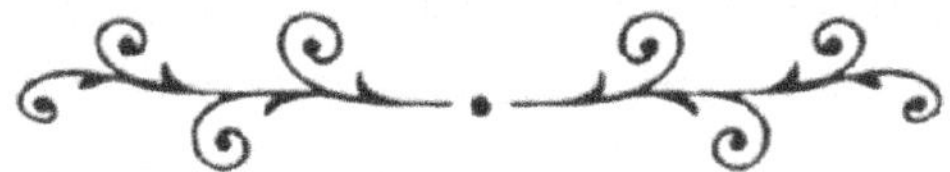

Lucas seemed to have decided to talk to Courtney already.

Aria watched as he walked over to her and gently drew her aside. She hoped he wouldn't say anything about her pregnancy.

His hand rested on her shoulder, and she looked down at her clipboard, shaking her head. They spoke some more, both looking earnest. Serious.

Aria couldn't hear what they were saying, but then Courtney smiled and looked up at him. Gave him a hug. Lucas patted her on the back, then pulled back his hands, holding her shoulders as he said something else to her.

If it wasn't for the fact that her sister-in-law was happily married to her brother, Aria might have felt a little jealous at how attentive Lucas was.

Which bothered her more than she wanted to admit.

Then Courtney joined the group, looking much happier than she had a few moments ago.

"Okay, people, this is the dance scene, and I hope you all remember your steps," Courtney announced, looking everyone over.

As she took her position, Lucas joined her, tucking his arm into Aria's, as was required. It was part of the play, but she couldn't stop a faint tug in her midsection at his touch.

She closed her eyes for a moment to center herself, but even as she drew up her defenses, the few looks they shared wafted on the edges of her thoughts. The surprise and the faint kindling of appeal she felt when she had impulsively touched his shoulder. The way his eyes softened and clung to hers.

She knew she wasn't imagining the connection that arced between them.

What was going on? What was he doing?

Then Courtney was giving instructions again, and they were caught up in the movements, concentrating. Aria stumbled when Kip accidentally stepped on her foot during an allemande left, the last one. She might have fallen, but Lucas caught her and, to cover up, picked her up and swung her around, settling her down beside him.

"Um, that's not in the script," Courtney called out from her position beside the square dance caller.

"Improvising. Some of the best scenes happen that way," Lucas returned.

Courtney just shook her head, as if admitting that she couldn't control Lucas either.

They ran through the sequence once more, and as Aria danced around the set to join Lucas, she waggled a warning finger at him. Though he grinned at her, thankfully he stuck to what he was supposed to do.

Courtney was satisfied with the dance practice, so she told them to skip back to one of the earlier scenes, which had caused trouble for Aria and Grady. Aria was surprised at the choice. She thought Courtney would want to wait until Grady returned to review the scene.

Dismissing her questions, she took her spot in the quickly improvised dining room. In the scene, Elizabeth had visited

Netherfield to check on Jane, who had taken ill, and Miss Bingley forced Elizabeth to take a turn around the room with her. Except the room wasn't a fancy drawing room – it was simply a barn – and Mr. Darcy was braiding a rope instead of writing a letter.

"Will you not join us, Mr. Darcy?" Stephanie asked, pretending to flirt with him.

Lucas dropped his rope and jumped to his feet. "Nothing I'd love more than to perambulate around the barn with two such lovely women."

"Cut. Cut. Darcy is supposed to be aloof."

Lucas frowned, looking down at the script. "I dunno. A few lines down, it looks like Elizabeth and Stephanie, I mean Miss Bingley, will be teasing him."

"And you can't take a little teasing?" Aria bantered.

"I can, but only if it's direct. This seems kind of, well, mean."

"Please. Just go with the script." Courtney turned to RayAnn, who had joined them. "I have to check on a few other things, can you make sure these people do what they're supposed to?"

"Sure, I guess?" RayAnn took a script from Courtney and looked over the group. "But I don't know if Lucas will listen to me."

"I'll try, little sis." Lucas grinned at her, then took his place again.

They ran through the next few lines, and thankfully Lucas followed the script to the letter.

Until it came to the point where Elizabeth and Darcy began exchanging barbs.

"So, is he? A man without fault?" Aria asked Stephanie, who was playing Miss Bingley, as she gave Lucas the slightly mocking look the script called for.

Again, Lucas held her gaze, and without looking at the script, spoke the lines. "No such thing. Every man has faults.

But I've tried to avoid weakness. Tried to make myself a better person where I can, so I can't be ridiculed. So, I can be proud of who I am, though I've made mistakes along the way."

The words were not in the script. More of an ad lib. But the seriousness in his face gave her pause.

Subtext?

She took a quick breath and carried on with her lines. "That sounds a lot like pride and vanity." Though it really didn't, but she wasn't sure what else to say.

Lucas shrugged. "Vanity, yeah. That's not cool." Then he flicked his hand through his hair. "Though when you've got something to be vain about…"

"And you do?"

"Well, yeah. This hair. I mean, c'mon. And all natural."

"If that's important to you," she continued. She stifled a chuckle, glanced quickly at the script, trying to find her place, trying to bring it back to the theme of the play. "You still sound as if you're quite prideful to me," she returned.

"I can be. But I can tell you, getting up from an arena floor with dust in your mouth knocks some of that pride away."

"Though you were always proud of your winnings and achievements."

"I was, but I also knew how they happened. Because of your father."

Even in this play, he managed to bring her father into the picture. The man Lucas had admired so much. The man whose memory she fought to leave behind every day.

"Um guys, that's not what it says you're supposed to do," RayAnn admonished. "You need to stick to the script."

"Okay, mini Courtney. I'll try to behave," Lucas replied with a mock salute.

Thankfully he was as good as his word, and once again they followed the script.

To her surprise, he could turn on the seriousness when

asked for, and despite RayAnn being his little sister, he listened to her and did what she asked.

When they were done the scene, he walked over to RayAnn, slung his arm over her shoulder, and gave her a quick one-armed hug.

Aria was close enough to hear what they spoke about. Lucas' relationship with his family had always intrigued her. Though she and Cole were close, she had often yearned for a sister, younger or older, with whom she could share confidences. Talk about her relationship with Lucas. A relationship that she had fallen headfirst into, without holding back. Lucas had known exactly how to capture her heart, making her hand it over to him without reservation.

Until he tossed it back at her, broken and ragged.

Aria spun away and strode across the room.

Grady couldn't come back fast enough.

But then Courtney called out her name, stopping her midstride. She turned to join her sister-in-law and brother, who were perched on a sawhorse, looking over some papers.

"Hey, Aria. How did that last scene go?"

"Once we got Lucas' ad-libbing under control, pretty good."

"He's a fast learner."

"I suppose." Right now, she was too confused about him to give him much more than lukewarm praise. "Though I'll be glad when Grady comes back."

That would make it much easier for her.

"Well, about that." Courtney bit her lip, and Aria felt a flicker of concern.

"Grady just called. His mother is worse than he thought, and he won't have time to come to practice. He's coming back tomorrow, but the next while he's going to be traveling back and forth to help his mom when he can. I think Lucas will have to take over permanently."

Aria just stared at Courtney then shook her head. "Of course. I understand."

"It's just a play. You'll be fine," Cole returned, his voice holding just enough concern to understand where she was coming from, and yet a firmness that reminded her how she'd weathered tougher storms than this.

"Yeah. I will be. Thanks." She gave Cole a smile to show him she understood, then walked over to get herself a coffee.

As she drank it, she couldn't help turning just enough to see Lucas sitting down with RayAnn, who looked upset. He had his hand on her shoulder, consoling her.

He was a good man, despite his protestations a few moments ago.

One of these days, she would be able to see him as just a man.

One day.

LUCAS TAPPED his fingers on the steering wheel of the truck, keeping time with the music and enjoying the spring sun, which filtered through the trees arching over the quiet residential street. It was a good day and only going to get better.

As soon as he got back to the ranch, he and Burke were heading over to the Waldren ranch with the horses to ride fence there for the rest of the day.

He slowed, turned a corner, then hit the brakes and swerved, skimming past a woman jogging down the middle of the street.

As he passed her, he saw a couple walking with a stroller, a dog trotting alongside them, that she was obviously avoiding.

That was Aria, he realized, glancing at the woman in his rear-view mirror. Slim, long golden hair pulled back in a ponytail that bobbed as she ran.

He was about to look away when the dog pulled at his leash, popped it out of his owner's hands, and ran after Aria.

Lucas slowed as he watched, then stopped as the dog jumped on Aria. She fell, her hands out in front of her just as the man came running toward her and the dog.

Lucas slammed on the brakes, shoved the truck in park and jumped out, running toward Aria, who was lying down on the road, the dog standing over her.

"Get that dog away from her," Lucas called out, waving at the owner, who was trying to catch his wayward pet.

The dog noticed Lucas and, distracted, came running toward him, ears flapping.

"No, you don't," Lucas growled, stepping on the leash as the dog ran past him. The dog jerked to a halt, then stood, looking at him. He bent down, grabbed the leash, and handed it to the owner, who apologized profusely.

Lucas didn't recognize him, but the woman, who was now bending over Aria, was Jenna Burke.

But right now, his concern was for Aria. He ran to her side, bending down just as she scrambled to get up, crying out in pain.

"What hurts?" he asked, lifting her up to a sitting position.

"My wrist, my leg," she groaned, blowing out her breath on a sigh of pain.

"I'm so sorry. I didn't think he'd get away that quick." The man had returned with the dog and was approaching them.

"Keep that dog away," Lucas warned, unable to keep the sharp tone out of his voice as Aria covered her head with her arms.

Aria was terrified of dogs. A stray dog had entered their yard one day while their father was at a rodeo for the weekend. It saw Aria and went directly for her. Cole fought to pull the dog off, but it was a traumatic struggle.

Aria had ended up in the hospital and needed ten stitches

in her upper leg. The dog was taken to the veterinarian and put down.

She never trusted dogs after that.

"I'm sorry. I'm so, so sorry." Jenna apologized. Her child was crying, and the dog was pulling at his leash.

The dog was simply being playful, but Aria was cowering on the street.

"I know, but please, just take the dog away."

"Is she going to be okay?"

"I'll take care of it. Please, just go. It'll be fine."

Lucas supported Aria, waving at Jenna and her husband to leave. They finally got the message, and with another flurry of apologies, they walked away, glancing back as they did so, obviously reluctant to leave Aria alone.

"Is it gone?" Aria asked, her voice wavering.

"Yes. It's okay. I'm here." His heart broke for her, knowing her pride would have a hard time with him seeing her like this. "Can you stand up? I should take you to the hospital."

"No. Don't. I'll be fine." But even as she pushed him away, a cry of pain wrenched out of her.

"I think you hurt your wrist when you fell."

"Please, just leave me alone."

He sat back on his heels, watching as she struggled to her feet, then wavered.

He jumped up, catching her by the waist before she fell again. She let out another cry of pain, and Lucas made a quick decision. Ignoring her protests, he bent, fitted his arms under her knees, lifted her up, and walked with her back to the truck.

She struggled, as he figured she would. "Just let me go back to my apartment. I'm fine."

"Look, you keep fighting, and we're both going down. I'll throw my titanium shoulder out, and everything will go to pot then."

By the time he had gasped out his little speech, he was

back at the truck, and she was frowning at him, obviously distracted.

"You don't have a titanium shoulder."

"How do you know I don't?" he asked, as he let go of her for a moment to open his truck's door.

She winced again, and he opened the door, holding her with one arm, as if afraid she would escape, then he fitted his arm under her knees, lifted her, and set her on the front seat of his truck.

Her lack of protest and the way she was cradling her arm showed him that her injury was worse than she would admit. He pulled on the seat belt and, reaching across her, buckled her in. The simple motion felt caring and intimate. The weak smile she gave him only cemented the impression.

He touched her shoulder in assurance. "It'll all be okay," he promised.

"Do you really think so?"

He held her eyes, wondering what she was referring to, thinking about the few times he had sensed a hint of the emotions they once shared. He couldn't look away as his mind shifted back to that horrible time when he had walked away from her.

You had a good reason, he reminded himself.

But her father was gone, and Lucas was back and buying her father's ranch.

Could something happen between them again? Did he dare hope she would forgive him?

Then she looked away, leaning her head back against the truck seat, and he pulled himself back to the task at hand. He carefully closed the door, jogged around the front of the truck, climbed in, and headed to the hospital.

Chapter 8

"You're lucky you didn't break your arm," Liam announced, checking out the x-ray as Aria leaned back on the bed in the Emergency Department. The ward nurse had put her in the trauma room, and she was thankful for the privacy.

Lucas had insisted on staying with her, and she wasn't sure how to feel about that.

"So, what's the verdict?"

"Will she be able to play the violin again?" Lucas asked.

"Sure. But not until the sprain heals." Liam sounded puzzled, and Aria wondered what Lucas was getting at.

"That's great, because she couldn't before."

Aria just rolled her eyes and sent Liam a mocking look. "That's your brother?" she asked him.

"Trust me, I had nothing to do with his upbringing. Out of my wheelhouse." Then Liam became more serious. "So, yeah, it's a sprain. Tensor bandage, hot and cold compresses. Take Advil for pain as needed and stay away from your computer for a couple of days if you can."

Thankfully, it was Saturday. She should be better by Monday.

"As for your ankle, it's fine. Just badly bruised when you fell. Again, I'd recommend keeping it elevated for a day or so. Just to be on the safe side."

"Okay. Thanks so much." Aria carefully shifted, lowering her legs to the floor, wincing as she did so. Liam had said it was just bruised, but it felt worse than that. Though, if she were honest, her pride had taken the biggest beating. Falling on the pavement. Having Lucas rescue her.

Being so stupidly afraid of a labradoodle, the easiest going dog breed alive.

She tried to stand, wavering.

Then, to her consternation, Lucas was right there beside her, holding her up. "Does she need anything else?" Lucas asked his brother.

Liam just shook his head. "Nope. Just make sure she rests up and doesn't overdo it."

"I think I can manage that on my own," she declared, a sharp note in her voice. They were talking about her as if she couldn't do this herself.

"Of course, you can," Liam agreed with a sheepish look.

Despite her protest, Lucas didn't move from her side as she started to walk, and he supported her as they made their way out of the Emergency Department. She wanted to pull away, but her leg hurt enough that she appreciated his assistance. All she wanted, however, was to get home, have a shower, and feel sorry for herself in her comfy chair.

Once again, Lucas helped her into his truck, but this time she buckled herself in, awkward as it was using her left hand.

A few minutes later, he escorted her into her apartment. She was glad she'd cleaned it before she went jogging, though a pile of papers still sat on her desk by the patio doors. A hoodie hung off the screen of her exercise bike, a remnant of her workout last night.

"Don't think you'll be riding that bike anytime soon," Lucas observed. Then he paused. "Where do you want to sit?"

"I want to take a shower." She grimaced down at her pants, the knees holding bloodstains from the scratches she'd gotten when she fell onto the pavement.

"I understand."

Aria sent a frown his way as he started walking her down the hall to the bathroom off her bedroom.

"I'm okay. You can go home now," she grumbled.

"I think I'll wait around. Just to make sure you don't fall again."

She wasn't keen on the idea of him sticking around while she showered, but she didn't have the energy to fight him. Her knee throbbed, her wrist ached, and her body felt every jolt she had experienced when she fell.

She hobbled into the bedroom and closed the door on him.

It took her longer than normal, but once she was done, and had replaced the tensor bandage, she opened the door of her bedroom to find him waiting at the end of the hall.

"I made you some tea and a snack," he offered with a faint smile. "Did you take the Advil Liam said you should?"

"Yeah, I did. I feel so much better already. It's a miracle. I'm fine."

He frowned at the faint sarcasm in her voice, and she couldn't help her own smile.

"I'm kidding," she said. "I'm sure it will take a while to kick in."

She put her hand against the wall to walk to the living room, knowing she should insist that he leave.

But despite her brain telling her the smart thing to do, the loneliness that had oppressed her over the last few days enjoyed having someone, anyone, spend some time with her. The idea that someone cared about what had happened to her felt comforting.

She eased herself carefully onto the loveseat and took the mug of tea he handed her with a smile of thanks. She put her foot up on the footstool he had set beside her chair. She took a sip and then shifted to put the mug onto the end table, but she forgot about the box that was there and accidentally knocked it over.

The contents spilled out onto the floor. Letters and papers.

From her father.

Lucas was right there, kneeling down, setting the box straight and picking up the envelopes, putting them back into the box.

Suddenly, he paused, holding one in his hand, then glanced up at her with a puzzled smile.

Aria could see the question on his face.

"Those are letters my dad and mom wrote to each other when they were dating."

"Really? That's cool."

"Yeah, I guess." She still wasn't sure what to make of what she read inside. A juxtaposition from her own memories. A drastic disconnect from Cole's. "I haven't had a chance to read them all."

"Really? Why not?" He put the lid back on the shoe box but set it on the coffee table between them. Probably so she couldn't knock it over again.

"I just got them last night."

"What? How did that happen?"

He took his own cup and settled down across from her on the couch, leaning forward in curiosity.

Aria glanced at the box, feeling, once again, the surge of bewilderment it created.

"The box came in the mail last night from our renter."

"And you just got them now? How did that work? Wouldn't you have known about them before?"

"I didn't know they existed."

Aria took a sip of tea, her mind going back to the week her father died.

Her father's death had been sudden and unexpected,

much like Lucas' parents' deaths had been when they happened six months earlier than her father's.

But while the church had been filled to overflowing for the Prins family, her father's funeral had been a stark, cold affair. He had chosen to be cremated and have no public service. Instead, it was just Aria and Cole burying an urn beside their mother's grave. Appropriately, it had been a bitterly wintry day.

Cole had left immediately afterward. Aria had stayed a few days longer, catching up with sympathetic friends, trying to figure out how she felt about the loss of a complicated father.

Then it was back to work in Vancouver.

"Apparently, the box was found on the top shelf of a closet in my dad's office. The company I hired to clean out the house after Dad died obviously missed it. The renters only used that room for storage, but the movers found it and apparently thought it belonged to the renters. They, in turn, sent it on to me."

She had read a few of the letters, unable to blend the man who wrote them with the man she remembered. The man Cole had told her more about the other day.

Which sent her out of the apartment to go running.

Which got her back here with a sprained wrist and twisted ankle.

With Lucas.

"That's kind of neat to have that memento. I'm sure it means a lot to you to be able to read them."

"It means something …" she let the sentence trail off, still fighting her confusion.

"I know for myself, it's been bittersweet coming back to Aspen Valley. Reliving memories of my parents, being in the house I grew up in."

He said nothing after that, as if waiting for her to participate. But she just sipped her tea, letting the moment settle.

Lucas said nothing more.

But to her surprise, the stillness wasn't awkward, despite the box of her father's letters sitting between them. Aria thought of other times she and Lucas had spent together, content to just be around each other.

Her mind slipped back to a day when they took his family's canoe out to a secluded spot on the lake. They ate some sandwiches she'd made. When they were done, she lay with her head in his lap, as they each read.

"You okay? You look kind of sad," Lucas asked.

She glanced over at him, not surprised. Lucas always had that ability to read her moods.

And now, suddenly, she was tired of the constant memories he recreated, the emotions she wanted to be done with. She needed some answers.

Maybe it was slipping into her father's past. Maybe it was a need to find her way to the present. She needed to know.

Straightening her shoulders and lifting her chin, she prepared herself, as she did in law school when she had to make a presentation. Or argue a case in fake court.

But this wasn't some case from which she had to keep herself emotionally removed. This was the man who had meant everything to her. Years ago, admittedly, but she hadn't met anyone else who made her feel the way Lucas had.

You're an adult. Get over it.

"You know, ever since you've come back," she began, "there's been this awkwardness I feel around you, and I'm tired of feeling that way."

That caught his attention.

"This may seem like delving into a past I should have moved on from, but now I'm just curious." It was more than that, but no sense letting Lucas know how deeply his leaving had wounded her. "Why did you break up with me all those years ago?"

To her surprise, Lucas didn't smile, didn't tease her. Didn't shrug off her question. Instead, he was quiet, as if weighing her question.

He pulled in a long breath and rested his elbows on his knees, his mug clutched in his hands.

"I guess I did it because I thought I should." Again, a beat to let his comment rest in the silence that rose up.

"What do you mean?"

He set his mug on the table, looking directly at her, his eyes boring into hers.

"Because I knew what I was. A broke cowboy who idolized your father. Who cared deeply about you. Who had precious little to offer you."

She wasn't sure what bothered her more. His comment about her father or his comment about his feelings being in the past tense.

She sat back, cradling her arm. Trying not to let too much ride on his answer. "Why did you think that?"

"You were a Waldren. Your family always had way more land, more cattle, more money than my family did. Than many people did, actually. You always had the best clothes, the nicest vehicles. Your house was a showpiece, your dad's arena was world class. Your dad was a legend in rodeo circles. That was a tough act to follow on every level."

She wanted to protest that she had never asked him to follow it, but, again, chose to wait. Something she'd always had a hard time with during law school and in some of her cases. She had eventually learned when to push, hoping the person she was examining would get flustered and flounder, when to wait and let them fill the silence with words they might later regret.

This was a time to wait.

"I knew I couldn't give you what you father did or be the person your father was. I cared so much for you, and I didn't want you to end up resenting how little I could give you."

She frowned at that and couldn't keep quiet anymore. "I

never asked you to give me what my father did. I never expected that."

"No, you didn't. But I know how my parents struggled because of unpaid bills. Money they lost. When money was tight, they had fights. They had hard times, and I knew I didn't want that in my future." He bit his lip, as if ashamed to even bring up his family's past.

"But your parents seemed to genuinely love each other," Aria pointed out, puzzled.

"They did. My parents got through it. But it was thanks to Shelby sticking around for a while and supporting them. She had failed Grade Twelve and decided to stay in Aspen Valley. I didn't know what was happening at the time. I had other priorities." He held her gaze at that, and she knew he was referring to the many times they sat up in the hayloft of the barn on their farm, talking about their future. He was going to be a rodeo star. She was going to school to become a lawyer. She wanted to move away. He wanted to stay. It was one of the points of contention between them.

"So many plans," she said with a crooked smile.

"Things were simpler, and I thought love would be enough for both of us. But I was just dreaming. Your father was a man I deeply respected. He taught me so much, and not just about rodeoing. About life and learning to fail. He was a mentor in so many ways. Though I had my own father, he and I never really saw eye to eye on the passion I had for rodeo. And that's where your dad came in." Lucas eyes shifted past her as if remembering.

Once again, Aria struggled with the disparity between Lucas' perception of her father and her own memories. It was a complicated relationship.

Lucas looked back at her again, his mouth still holding that half-smile. "I respected him. A lot. So, when he talked about my relationship with you, well, I listened."

"What do you mean? When did you talk to him about us?"

She and Lucas had always been so secretive. She didn't want her father to know about her relationship with Lucas because she didn't want him to criticize it, take it apart. It was bad enough that she had to hear from him how her clothes were too revealing, her makeup not subdued enough. He always said it was because he didn't want her besmirching the Waldren name and history. As if her crop-tops and eyeliner were weapons in a cultural war she wasn't even fighting.

And given what she had found out from Cole, her anger against him was rekindled.

Lucas folded his hands, tapping his thumbs together, his lips pursed, then he blew out a sigh and looked up at her.

"I talked to your dad when I was going to ask if he would give me his blessing to marry you."

Aria saw his lips move, heard his words on one level, but they didn't register immediately. It took a few thumps of her heart before she processed what he said before the words "marry me."

"You were going to propose?" Her voice came out small, sounding insignificant, and it made her angry he still has this effect on her.

"Yes. And I wanted his blessing."

"So…what happened?" Because, obviously, he hadn't proposed. Instead, he did the complete opposite by breaking up with her and leaving.

He chewed one corner of his mouth, as if weighing what to tell her. "What happened?" he repeated. "I'll tell you. After your father got over his anger over our 'sneaking around' as he called it, he told me I had disappointed him. That he couldn't believe we had acted the way we had. He made me feel ashamed."

"Of what? Of me?"

"No. Never of you. But how I had betrayed his trust."

"How did he think you had done that?" She couldn't wrap her head around what he was saying.

"He shared his knowledge with me. Had spent so much time with me. So, yeah, I felt like I had done something wrong by hiding our relationship from him."

"You were dating me, not him." Aria struggled to follow along. Usually, she kept up with a line of questioning. But usually, she knew the answers before she asked them. The lawyer's number one rule.

But this, this was new, uncharted territory, and she was floundering.

"The kicker came when he told me that you were too good for me," Lucas continued. "Said that I couldn't offer you the life he could. He said exactly what I'd been thinking."

"I told you, I didn't want that."

"Maybe. But I knew who I was and what I had to offer you. When your dad asked me to leave you alone, I respected him too much to argue."

"So, you listened to my father?" Her heart twisted at the thought. "You didn't think you should talk to me?"

Lucas looked away, as if unable to face her. "I wanted to, but your father told me not to come by anymore. That I couldn't be trusted. And then, the next day, as I was leaving town, I saw you driving down the street in a brand-new convertible. And it was as if that moment encapsulated everything your dad had said to me."

Aria could say nothing for a moment, then blew out a hard sigh. "That's why he bought that car. I thought it was an early birthday present. At least that's what he told me."

She let the thoughts digest, her anger with her father rising. Again.

"You need to know, I respected you as much as I respected your father," Lucas continued. "But I had second thoughts until I saw Drew Rozak beside you in your fancy car. Son of one of the richest men in Aspen Valley. I knew not only that I couldn't give you what your father did, but I also couldn't give you what Drew could."

"I didn't ask for the car, and Drew was…is…an old family friend," she said, keeping her voice even. She had nothing to apologize for. "Our parents always hoped we would end up together."

"And that happened."

"Only because of our shared history. After you left, he asked me out. He was easy to be around." She stopped there, knowing she didn't need to explain herself, yet she realized how dating Drew after they broke up would have looked to him.

The Rozaks had a home in what was nicknamed The Golden Ring, the fancy part of town. They also owned a villa in Italy. Mr. Rozak was an insurance broker. Drew had attended law school and hadn't had to pay for anything.

She could see how the situation might have looked to Lucas.

"Anyway, between those two events and what your father said, I felt stuck."

"My father…"Aria closed her eyes, resting her head against the back of her love seat, her feelings so conflicted she wasn't even sure how to express them. How could her father have done this? And why did Lucas believe him?

Because you took everything your father ever gave you and saw it as your due.

Her head was tired, and her arm ached. Her heart was still dealing with what Lucas had told her. It was too much. The pain, the information she had just received, her own emotions about her father. She just wanted it all gone. Done.

To her frustration, she felt a sob claw up her throat and then the confusing tears pooled behind her eyelids.

No. She wasn't going to cry. She wasn't.

LUCAS WANTED to keep his distance, but when the glistening track of a tear slid down Aria's cheek, he crossed the room and sat beside her. Her silent sorrow over losing her father was like an arrow in his heart.

He cupped her face with one hand, his thumb brushing the tears from her cheek.

"Hey, it's hard. I know what losing a parent feels like." He wasn't just mouthing platitudes. He really did. His own parents had been taken too soon.

To his surprise, she reached up and caught his wrist, her delicate fingers circling it. For a moment, he thought she would push it away. Instead, she kept a firm grip, holding it fast.

His gaze entangled with hers, and his breath lodged in his throat at the sight of her glistening, blue eyes.

He tried to ground himself back into reality. But all the dreams he'd spun around this girl, the yearnings he'd had to push down for so long, infiltrated his wounded and lonely heart.

When she didn't look away, when he saw the trembling of her lips and the faint movement of her face toward him, his hand eased behind her neck, shifting her closer.

Their breath mingled, their lips brushed each other. Hesitantly at first, then memory and old rhythms returned, and her hand was anchoring his head, their mouths slipping, moving over each other.

His heart beat a hard crescendo as he felt warmth, gentle connection, then heat and passion.

He knew he had to stop. This was not a good idea.

And yet…

She lowered her hand, drew back, looking down.

Should he apologize for something he'd been dreaming of doing ever since he saw her for the first time? Should he explain what he was thinking?

But she had seemed as willing as he was.

Whatever had instigated this, he knew there was no going back to where they were before.

But what would happen from here?

They were quiet a moment, as if letting their kiss find its way into the moment. Each adjusting their expectations of past and future.

Then she looked up at him. "You said you know what it feels like to lose a parent. And I know I didn't ever fully appreciate what you and your family had to deal with after your parents died. We weren't…weren't together, but I want to tell you that I grieved their passing, too."

He didn't want to return to the past. He wanted to touch her, to reconnect, but they both needed some space to process what had happened to them.

Instead, he followed her lead. "They liked you a lot."

"Even though Shelby thought I was a snob?"

Lucas shrugged off her question. "Shelby has always been way too protective of the family. Even before she had to take care of the twins, Celeste, and Jacob, she'd always been like a mother hen." He touched her hand, tracing the light veins, pale blue through her translucent skin. "She would never have admitted it, but I think she was jealous of how easy things were for you. And of how beautiful you were then and are now."

"Looks can be deceiving, and they certainly aren't everything." Then she tweaked out a tight smile. "But I'm more than this." She waved a hand in front of her face.

"I know that," he assured her. "I see you. I know who you are."

Then she smiled, shaking her head. "You always did, I think."

"You don't need to think. I know you used to get frustrated when people would tell you how good looking you are. How beautiful. I mean, the reality is, you are. You're stunning. But, like I said, I know who you are behind those porcelain features, those sapphire blue eyes, that golden blonde hair. I know your heart, and that always meant more to me than what you looked like."

"I dyed my hair once. When I was in law school. Just to try being someone different."

Lucas gave her a shocked look. "Really? What color?"

"Red. At least it was supposed to be red, not the heinous shade of orange it ended up being. I had to cut most of it off to get rid of it."

He couldn't help picking up a strand of her hair, running his fingers through its silky softness, reveling in the permission their shared kiss had given him

"That would have been interesting to see," he teased, his tone light. Gentle.

"Interesting is putting it kindly."

This time the weight of the quiet between them seemed easier.

"I just want to get back to what we were talking about," Lucas said. "I'm sorry you lost your dad. I understand how that can take the ground out from under you."

"Of course you do. You lost both your parents at once, and I know you all really cared about each other. What happened to me was –" she stopped there, looking past him through the large French doors of her apartment, to the sun now setting over the mountains, shining onto the lake.

"Was what?" he prompted.

She gave a light shake of her head, then turned back to him, taking his hand in hers, creating a light thrill that shivered up his back. "Nothing. My mind wandered for a moment. I was just glad Cole and I had each other and that you had your family."

"Too many of them at times," he agreed, giving her a cautious smile, feeling like she was going to say something else, but stopped herself.

He didn't want to follow up on it and bring anything else

into this moment they had shared. This tenuous link they had rebuilt. He wasn't sure where it was going, but for now, it was wonderful to be beside her.

"Maybe. But I've seen you with you Shelby, Liam, Burke, and the twins," she continued. "You're a good brother, and I think they feel the same about you."

"Thanks. Coming back has been an eye-opener. Getting dropped back into the family hasn't always been easy. The R's are older, Jacob is getting moody, and now Celeste and Nadia are talking about coming back. If they do, us guys will be outnumbered again."

"I'm sure you guys can handle yourself. I've seen you, Liam, and Burke in action."

"What you don't see is the behind-the-scenes planning. It's a constant war of attrition. Those girls can wear us down if we're not careful."

She chuckled, and he smiled at the sound.

It was like they had meandered back to the old give-and-take they used to enjoy.

"I just wish we'd had our dad around a little longer," Lucas commented. "I'm sure you feel the same, but I was thankful I could share him with you."

He caught the slight retreat, the ever so vague chill slip over her features.

An expression of her loss?

"My father meant a lot to you, didn't he?" Aria finally asked.

The yearning in her voice showed how she missed him. She and her father had been close. Lucas knew her brother Cole hadn't always gotten along with Steven. He knew it was a source of constant sorrow for their dad.

"He did," Lucas agreed. "Though I had a loving father, I have to admit, there were many times I saw Steven almost as a father figure as well. I respected and admired him. He taught me so much and gave me more than I could ever repay. He was generous with his time and advice." As memories bombarded him, Lucas had a hard time keeping the emotion out of his voice.

"You didn't come to my dad's funeral." Her comment held no acrimony that he could hear. It seemed to be a simple statement of fact.

Lucas tried not to let the shame of that time wash back over him. But he sensed that she needed to know.

"Much as I hate to admit it, that was at a very low point for me." He paused a moment, glancing around once more at the beautiful apartment where Aria lived. The spacious living space, the walnut kitchen cabinets, granite countertops. The gleaming hardwood floors. Floor to ceiling windows that led to a wide balcony overlooking the lake and the mountains beyond that, and below, a creek that fed into Aspen Lake.

It only served to remind him of how little he'd had to offer her then. Even though he was now purchasing her ranch, he still couldn't offer her much. He and Burke had talked about subdividing the house and yard and selling it to help finance the purchase of the ranch.

"Why was that?" Again, her voice was soft, curious.

He wanted to pull away and create some distance, but he didn't want to let go of her hand and break this sweet and tender connection between them.

Instead, he pulled in a deep breath, casting his mind back to that dark time.

"I was laid up in San Antonio, still healing from a broken leg. I couldn't drive and didn't know anyone willing to take me that far. It was hard not to be able to come."

"I did get the card you sent to me and Cole."

"Yeah, well, sorry about that." Even thinking about the cheap gas-station card he sent made him want to curl up in embarrassment.

"The thought was kind." She removed her hand from his. "So, what happened after that?"

Lucas clasped his hands together, leaning forward, turning to look at her. Her expression was impassive, and he couldn't read it. As if his confession had made her pull away from him.

"I felt like I had hit bottom when I couldn't even make it to the funeral of the man who had done so much for me. So, I decided I would honor him in other ways. I focused on my healing. Did my exercises. Worked hard so I could keep saving as well as sending money home."

"Wait, what do you mean, sending money home?" She touched his arm, as if to get his attention. He barely moved, liking the feel of her hand.

"After mom and dad died, there wasn't a ton of money left for Shelby to keep the farm going and take care of Jacob, Celeste, and the twins. Dad had made some bad financial decisions. Trusted the wrong person with his money." He could still get angry when he thought of how his father had been swindled. "Whoever could, sent money home to help out."

"That's incredible."

"What was incredible was the sacrifice Shelby made so she could take care of the kids. But we helped as much as possible. Even Nadia, who had taken off without telling anyone what she was doing or where she went, sent money when she could. But I was tapped. Thankfully, Liam was making decent money as a doctor, and he could spot me until I, literally, got back on my feet again. I threw myself back into practicing all the things your dad taught me. Riding in his honor, using the saddle he gave me. I started going to church. I found my center again. And I started winning. Good money. Enough to keep me going. I sent some back to Shelby and built up a stake for my own future."

"What made you come back to Aspen Valley?"

His fingers curled around hers. "I was tired of roaming around without roots. I wanted to come back to my family and settle down. Be part of the community. Go to the same church each Sunday." He couldn't help a quick sidelong glance. "Like you had always encouraged me."

Another silence settled between them, and he wondered if it was the last thing he'd said that created a problem for her.

He knew she didn't attend church, even though the Waldren family always had. It bothered him deeply, because she'd been the one who had, more than anyone, even his parents, shown him the benefits of church family and community, and of maintaining a relationship with his creator and savior.

How it enriched and enhanced his life and gave it purpose and meaning.

"I'm glad you found that helpful." She gave him a wan smile.

"You don't go to church anymore." He chose to frame it as a statement more than a question.

"Haven't since I came back here."

"Was it because Drew broke up with you?"

Aria gave him a wry smile and shook her head. "No. And for the record, Drew didn't break up with me. We both realized that we weren't meant for each other. We both…" her voice trailed off.

"You both what?" he encouraged.

She pressed her lips together, her hand tightening on his as she shook her head.

"Did you think of me while you were gone?"

Her question lodged in his heart. He wasn't sure what to say. But they were sitting together on her couch. He had just comforted her. Kissed her. The time for holding back was slipping away.

"All the time. I imagined myself many times coming back to town, challenging Drew Kozak to a duel - though he would be tough to beat. He's not a small guy. Telling your father that I loved you. And then I thought of what Drew and your father could give you, and I couldn't." He tightened his hand on hers.

She returned his pressure. "My father had no right to say what he did to you." The edge of anger in her voice gave him a small thrill. "And to be brutally honest, I thought we were close enough that I wish you would have come to me. I wish you would have given me the opportunity to make a choice."

On one level, Lucas knew she was right. And yet…

"You were getting ready to leave for university," he said. "I knew your schooling was a fantastic opportunity for you. I knew you wanted to prove to yourself and to the people around you that you were and are more than the beautiful blonde who was Frosh Queen and Rodeo Queen. I didn't want to jeopardize that."

"And us getting married might have?"

"I know it sounds arrogant to say this, but I have a feeling if we had, you wouldn't have wanted to go to school. For us to be apart."

She got up from the couch and walked to the window, staring out, silhouetted against the setting sun, her right arm supporting her left. Then she turned back to him, smiling. "Hard as it is to admit this, I think you were right. I probably wouldn't have gone to school. I'm glad for my education, but I'm sad." Their eyes met and held. "I'm sad about the time we lost."

Her words dove into his heart, pushing away all the second thoughts he'd had while they were apart. The worries about what she would be like when he came back.

He stood up and joined her, slipping his arm across her shoulders, pulling her against him.

"I am too."

He laid his head on hers, releasing a deep sigh as they both looked out over the town.

He didn't want to think too far ahead. Right here, right

now, this amazing woman was back in his arms. Moment by moment was the way to carry on.

But he also knew that this time around, he had to get things right. Because if he didn't…

Don't go there, he warned himself. *It will all be fine.*

She was the person he had always wanted to be with, and he hoped that she felt the same.

It would work out. It had to.

Chapter 9

Was this a good idea?

Aria got out of her car looking over at the church, watching families walking across the parking lot. She looked down at her white flats peeking out of her flowing linen pants. She brushed a hand over the simple aqua top she wore, adjusted the chains around her neck.

Simple, yet elegant. Her signature look since she graduated from law school.

Her father would approve.

She shook off that thought and then wondered what Lucas would think.

Neither of which matters, she reprimanded herself as she walked toward the front entrance of the church.

Trouble was that the steady barrage of pointers and comments from her father as she was growing up had been one of the hardest things to shuck off as she got older. She had spent so much time trying to please him it had become an ingrained habit.

Now she was fighting another battle between her father's voice, reminding her of the importance of attending church, and her own innate need to establish her independence apart from his voice.

But still she hesitated, letting the spring sun wash over her, the light breeze tease her hair.

"Hey, Aria. Good to see you."

She turned in time to see her brother and his wife Courtney walking toward them, Fenna dawdling behind them. Cole was grinning, his arm around Courtney's in a protective gesture.

They joined her, and Cole frowned when he saw the tensor bandage on her arm. "What happened?"

Aria waved off his question. "Just avoiding a run-in with an overly enthusiastic labradoodle while I was running yesterday."

"Did you see a doctor?" His concern was like a warm hug.

"Yes, Lucas took me." As soon as the words came out of her mouth, she wished she could pull them back.

Especially when she saw the frown on Cole's face deepen. Cole had gotten along well with Lucas, but when her brother found out that Lucas was the one to break off their relationship, Lucas became persona non grata in Cole's books. Her brother had always been fiercely protective of her. It was what got him into trouble from time to time.

"But it's just a sprain, and I'll be better by tomorrow. Just in time to get back to work."

"Are you sure you should?" Courtney put in. "Might not hurt to take an extra day off."

"I would, but I'm swamped."

"Which reminds me, we should come in some time and update our will," Courtney commented.

Aria forced herself to hold Courtney's eyes and not look down at her stomach. Of course, she wasn't showing yet, but still…

"Never hurts to stay on top of that," was all Aria replied.

Together they walked through the doors of the church, and as they entered, a shiver unfurled down Aria's back. The last time she was here was for her father's funeral. A difficult and emotional time.

She took a breath, clutching the strap of her purse as if for support. From the hallway beside them, she heard the chatter of voices.

"You okay?" Cole asked, picking up on her edginess.

"I'm fine." She wasn't, but what washed over her was far too complicated to discuss as people milled around them and Fenna complained about having to be here.

Courtney pulled her daughter aside, bending over as she spoke to her in Dutch.

"Can you figure out what they're talking about?" she asked Cole.

He glanced over, then shrugged. "I'm learning a little bit, but I don't need to understand to know Fenna doesn't like what Courtney is saying. She's been balky lately." Cole lowered his voice, moving closer to Aria. "She knows about the baby, and I think she's worried she'll be dethroned."

Aria had to chuckle at that. "Did you feel the same about me?"

Cole shrugged. "I wasn't as old as Fenna, but yeah, I remember being annoyed when it became obvious you were dad's favorite."

He was joking, but Aria felt a quiver of sorrow at the thought. "I didn't ask for it, just so you know. And it wasn't all wonderful."

"Oh, don't I know that," Cole agreed, growing serious. "But I'm really glad you came to church today. I think you'll appreciate our pastor. He's not the fire and brimstone guy we had before, that Dad liked so much."

"That's good to know. Though I never really knew what brimstone was. Still don't, actually."

Cole chuckled at that. "Guess he never wanted us to find out. That's why he warned us about avoiding it so often."

Courtney joined them, shaking her head.

"Everything okay?"

"Fenna doesn't want to join the kids' church, but she also doesn't want to sit with us." Courtney blew out a sigh. "Honestly, I wish I could figure her out. One minute she's clingy as all get out, the next she's pushing me away."

"She's at that awkward age," Cole said, adding a chuckle. "Too old for toddler temper tantrums, too young for hormones."

"I don't even want to know what that will be like."

Aria chuckled at the fear in Courtney's voice. "She'll be fine," Aria assured her. "I'm sure once the baby comes all will be well."

Courtney's eyes grew wide, and Aria clapped her hand to her mouth, glancing around to make sure no one else heard.

Then, to Aria's surprise, Courtney grinned. "I guess it was too much to expect to keep it to myself too much longer."

"Congratulations, by the way." Aria gave her sister-in-law a quick, one-armed hug. "I'm thrilled for you guys."

"I am too, though Fenna is trying to figure out what this will do to her single-child status."

Aria wanted to assure her, but then Fenna marched ahead of them all, forcing them to follow.

"That girl loves to control the narrative," Cole sighed.

Aria and Courtney followed her into the sanctuary. Fenna flopped into a pew, making sure she was right against the aisle. "You sit with me, please," she commanded Aria.

"I guess we can be thankful for the please," Cole muttered.

Aria did as she was told, feeling honored by the request, though she sensed it might have had more to do with Fenna creating a convenient buffer between her and Courtney than the pleasure of her aunt's company.

The pastor strode to the front of the church as the singing group at the front finished their song.

"Welcome to the service this beautiful Palm Sunday morning," he greeted, as the last notes of their song echoed through the large church building. "This is the day the Lord has made. Let us rejoice and be glad in it," he quoted. "And now we're going to begin with a worship song led by the young children."

The band struck up a song that Aria didn't recognize, and the congregation got to their feet just as the first wave of children came marching into the church, waving palm branches, singing their Hosannahs.

Aria watched, not recognizing any of the kids, though she saw Doria Brouwer herding one group of kids and RayAnn Prins and Desni DeVries herding another group, encouraging them as they sang, walked, and waved.

Finally, they were all gathered at the front, and Aria smiled at the sight of all those sweet young faces. The music switched to another song, and they threw everything into it. She envied their unbridled enthusiasm.

They finished up, and the applause rang through the building. Aria couldn't help a knead of discomfort. What would her father think of this?

Pretentious. Silly. Disrespectful.

She pushed out of her mind the words she knew he would voice if he were present. He was gone. His opinion didn't matter anymore.

She joined in, feeling a bit rebellious and, if she were honest, free.

As they sang the next song, Fenna asked if she and Aria could trade places. Aria agreed, but as she switched, she saw Lucas sitting with his family across the aisle and a few rows ahead of her. He couldn't see her, but she had an uninterrupted view of him.

She let her eyes linger on his wavy hair, worn longer, and his broad shoulders in the plain, tan shirt. He had one hand shoved into the back pocket of his blue jeans, looking far more relaxed than she felt.

They sang a few more songs and then worked their way through the liturgy, including a responsive reading of one of the Psalms. Aria read along, but her attention was now divided between what the pastor was saying and the man she had kissed only yesterday.

Last night she'd had a rough time sleeping, and it wasn't just because of the pain in her arm.

It was as if the kiss they had shared still lingered on her lips. The touch of his hand still warming her shoulder.

Second thoughts fluttered and spun through her mind. How could they backtrack from what they had done?

Did she want to?

Once again, anger with her father and his interference in her life bloomed. She closed her eyes as the pastor started talking.

She folded her arms in a defensive gesture, then winced as the movement created a twinge of pain.

Her mind drifted off, thinking about what she had to do this week at work. Set up a partnership agreement for a client. Sign off on a corporate buy out. Land Titles needed to be contacted.

Which made her think about Lucas, which made her glance his way again. He was sitting beside RayAnn, his arm resting on the back of the pew. He said something to his sister, gave her a brief hug, and smiled down at her. Then he leaned forward, looking intently at the pastor.

Which made her pay attention as well.

"Before Palm Sunday, before Jesus came into the city, his heart was full of sorrow, not only for what he had to face, but for his beloved people." Pastor Muller looked down at his Bible. "This passage has always struck me deeply. 'Oh Jerusalem, Jerusalem… how often I have longed to gather your children together, as a hen gathers her chicks under her wings,' I have always found that to be an interesting analogy." He paused, then looked up. "This is the savior of the world, Father and Lord, comparing his love to a hen with her chicks. Having grown up without a father, son of a single mother, I struggled to see God as a father. But this passage reminds me that we may see God in a different light. It allows us to see his love through the love of a mother for her young. This is important for so many people, not only for me, but for those to whom the word 'father' might create difficult memories."

Aria felt as if she had been struck by a jolt of electricity. The words of the pastor pulsed through her. It was as if he had looked into her very soul and found the truth of her estrangement from church, from faith.

From God.

Her own relationship with her father was a morass of disappointment and expectations. Happiness and sorrow.

Confusion.

And then to discover that her father hard warned Lucas to stay away. He had used Lucas' deep respect and admiration for him as a weapon, refusing to give his blessing to Lucas and Aria, essentially telling Lucas he wasn't good enough for her.

She pulled in a shaky breath, forcing her attention back to the pastor.

"'Father' can be a loaded word for many of us, but it's good to see God through other eyes. To look past the language and know that he watches over the sparrow, that he has numbered the hairs on our head. That throughout the story of salvation, he stoops, and stoops, and stoops, coming down to our level. And, especially at Easter, to know how low he has come. To die for us. To take on our guilt and blame. This is love in its purest form. This sacrifice."

Aria sat back, as the pastor's sincerity came through with what he was saying. It was as if the love he spoke of trickled into her soul. A slow, gentle movement.

She unclenched a fist she didn't remember making, letting

her fingers fall open as if to better receive what God was offering.

The rest of what he said was lost on her, but she knew that something profound had happened in this moment. Something she would never forget.

As they stood for the parting song, she caught Cole glancing sidelong at her, concerned. She gave him an encouraging smile, hoping he wouldn't ask her anything more. Right now, all she wanted was to hold this moment close, save it for a time when she knew she might need it again.

"HEY, GIRL, WAIT UP," Lucas called out as Aria walked across the parking lot.

When RayAnn had told him she saw Aria in church, he went looking for her as soon as it was over.

As she turned, he thought he glimpsed sorrow on her face, but when he joined her, he wondered if he had imagined it.

"How's the arm?" he asked, pointing to the tensor bandage.

"It's still sore but getting better."

"You sleep okay last night?"

Her tranquil smile wrapped around his heart. "I did. Better than I have in a while."

He looked into her eyes, their bright pools holding the promise of a future. But he pulled back, reminding himself to move slowly. Let her take the lead.

"What's up for you the rest of the day?" He kept his tone casual. Just asking…

"I'm going to Cole and Courtney's for lunch, and then Brooke and I are going for a long-overdue walk together." She gave him a benevolent smile. "And what about you?"

"The usual. Dinner with the family at Burke and Karissa's.

They're on the home place now. Then I think I'll take one of the horses out for a ride. They need some exercise."

"That sounds like fun."

He remembered riding with her when he would come to her farm. Her father had some high-performance horses that they didn't go near, some bucking stock that he provided to rodeos, and a couple of horses that Cole and Aria used to ride when they were younger.

"Where did all your horses go?" he asked.

"Cole took care of selling them. He made sure that Daisy and Sherman went to good homes. The rest I didn't care about."

"If you ever want to go riding again, just say the word. We've got some great trails that we've been maintaining that go up into the hills. Pretty views. And it's pretty isolated."

She flashed a coy smile. "And what are you trying to say?"

He glanced around the parking lot. It was almost empty now. As far as he could see, his family members were gone. So, he moved a little closer. He wanted to kiss her, but a few people lingered, chatting.

"I'm just saying it would be nice to spend some time together out in God's beautiful creation."

"I would have to agree. I haven't been riding in a long time, and I've missed it." She held up her arm. "Though I would have to wait until this is completely healed."

"Of course." He paused a moment, allowing himself to appreciate the absolute ordinariness of the conversation. But he had another reason for stopping her. " I'm wondering whether your arm will be officially healed in time to do some dancing this Friday night? The Prairie Wanderers are doing a gig at the Roadhouse Grill in Edmonton, and I haven't been dancing in ages."

"Not so sure I still know how."

"I'm sure you'll pick up your rhythm in no time."

She smiled at that, then, to his pleasant surprise, nodded.

"I'd like that. Maybe we could bust out some square-dancing steps."

He held up one hand. "Please. No. It's bad enough we have to do that for the play."

"Do you have your lines memorized for Tuesday?"

He feigned a shocked look. "Tuesday night? Already? I thought our next practice wasn't until Thursday."

"Time's a ticking. Courtney is holding three practices a week from now until opening night."

"Ooh, boy. I'll have to break it to Burke that I won't be around much in the next few weeks."

"He knows."

"Okay then. I didn't go over the lines much." Then he had an idea. "Hey. Can I come over tomorrow night? We can run lines together. I'll take you out to the Pasta Place after."

"That's an offer I can't refuse."

Out of the corner of his eye, he saw the last vehicle leave the parking lot, and they were finally alone. He waited a moment, then resting his hand on her waist, gave her a gentle pull.

She didn't resist and stepped into his arms easily and willingly. He was careful not to jostle her wrist as he slipped his arm around her. "I've been wanting to do this ever since I saw you."

"In church?"

"Yeah. I guess." He grew serious, his hand making gentle circles over her lower back, sliding over the silk of her blouse, his calluses catching on it. "I was glad to see you here."

She ducked her head, her one hand curling up on his chest. "I'm glad…glad I came. It was harder than I thought, and I had to force myself to come."

This surprised him. When they were dating, she was the one who had always encouraged him to attend. Her reluctance to attend was puzzling.

"Why?"

Her only answer was a sigh, then she looked up at him, smiling, though he could see it was forced. "Doesn't matter. I enjoyed listening to Pastor Muller. I've never heard him preach before."

"The family seems to like him. He's down to earth. Apparently, he doesn't even mind hanging around with the Coffin Cheaters at the Grill and Chill."

"That almost makes him eligible for sainthood."

Lucas chuckled at that. "I doubt he would agree, but I think it's admirable."

Silence followed, a restful quiet counterpointed by birds singing, the whisper of tires over pavement, a burst of laughter from a house adjacent to the church.

Then she placed her hand on his chest, looking up at him. "You should probably go. I'm sure your family is waiting. I have something…something I need to do. By myself."

He wanted to ask what, but then she twined her hand around his neck, pulled him down and brushed a warm, soft kiss over his mouth.

He was about to pull her closer, but she deftly sidestepped him. "See you tomorrow," was all she said with a wave of her hand.

Curious, he watched her, but she went past her car and walked through the grove of trees separating the church from the graveyard.

Visiting her father's grave?

He watched her for a moment as she wended her way through the headstones, then stopped at a large, pink granite one.

You should go, he thought, yet he couldn't look away.

She stood in front of the gravesite, head bowed, arms wrapped around her middle. He remembered that her parents were buried side by side. Was it her mother she was remembering? Or her father?

Just as he was about to leave, he saw her drop to her knees, resting back on her heels, staring at the stone. Then she covered her face in her hands.

He wanted to rush to her side and comfort her, but he sensed that she needed to be alone.

Instead, he pushed down his mixed emotions, got into his truck, and with one last look back, he drove away.

Chapter 10

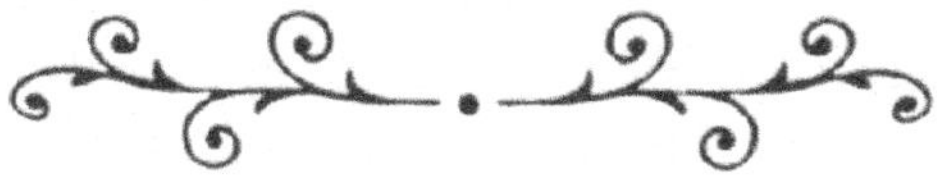

"You've got these lines down pat." Aria gave Lucas a quick smile.

Lucas had come to her place almost two hours ago, and they'd been going over their lines since then. They had done them standing up, but were now sitting on the couch, drinking the tea Aria had made. Lucas had devoured the cookies, claiming he had eaten little that day. He and Burke had been busy working on fences.

She thought of all the work needed on her father's ranch and tried not to feel a twinge of melancholy that the place she'd grown up on would no longer be accessible to her.

Then she glanced at Lucas, who was smiling over at her, and the tiniest tendril of possibility snaked into her thoughts.

She wanted to let it grow but didn't dare. For now, this was today, and she and Lucas were enjoying being together.

It was nothing more than that.

"Got lots of help from RayAnn and Roxie with the lines. They're such romantics at heart. It wasn't hard to get them to help me. They're desperately enamored of Regency romances, as they like to say."

Aria grinned at that. "Desperately enamored? That sounds like something right out of a Jane Austen book."

"Yeah. They were born out of time, though I keep trying to tell them that if they were born in the Regency era, they'd be poor scullery maids rather than ladies going out for tea and being presented to the Queen."

"Why would you want to burst their bubble like that?"

Lucas shrugged, scratching his temple with a forefinger. Something he used to do when they were dating. "It's called a reality check. Sometimes they need that."

Aria took a sip of her tea, leaning back on the couch cushions. "You get along well with your sisters, don't you?" She thought of the many interactions she'd seen of the three of them.

"I do, but not going to lie. I'm looking forward to getting my own place. I give Burke and Karissa a lot of credit for being such loving guardians for the kids."

"You and your family have had to deal with some difficult times." Aria took another sip of her tea, trying to stifle a tiny barb of jealousy. She and Cole hadn't always been so close, and much of it had to do with the breakdown of their family after their mother died. Cole had retreated into his own space, and she had felt abandoned, floundering along on her own, trying to sort out her own relationship with her father.

And often feeling caught between her brother and father.

"We have, but it's amazing how you can pull together when you have to." Lucas gave her a self-deprecating smile. "I know I haven't always been as emotionally supportive as I could have been, but I'm thankful I'm here now so I can help where I can."

"You know what, I'm glad you're here too."

Lucas's smile shifted, and he leaned closer, pressing his forehead against hers. "And I'm glad to hear that."

They sat like that for a moment, and she was thankful for the low-key interaction.

Then she drew back. "I guess we should get to the end of the next scene."

"You're quite the taskmaster. You could give Courtney a run for her money."

"Pass." She made a point of pulling out her papers and turning to the scene she had been talking about.

Lucas pulled out his own script and made a face as he skimmed it. "I guess this is the scene where Mr. Darcy shows up after his ill-advised swim in the lake. Not so sure I want to show up on the stage soaking wet."

Aria laughed at his pained expression. "I don't think Courtney is going for a scene-by-scene re-enactment. This is just the spot where Darcy is surprised at Lizzie's presence at his place." Then she couldn't resist a teasing comment. "Though it would be interesting to see you in a wet shirt."

"Now, now, this is a PG play." Then he returned her smile. "But if you come riding with me one day, I'm sure I can figure something out for you."

"Anyhow," she drew the word out to keep her mind from going to the thought of Lucas in a wet shirt. "Back to the script."

"Gotcha. Well, I always found this an interesting scene. Poor guy goes for a dip on his own property and ends up all deshabille in front of Miss Bennet?"

"What did you just say?" She lifted her eyebrows in surprise not only at the word, but his perfect pronunciation.

"It's not a bad word, in case you're going there. It's French."

"I know that. I didn't think you knew what it meant."

"I'm not a complete idiot. Just an incomplete one."

This made her laugh again. It had always been so easy with Lucas. She had missed this. Even with Drew, whom she had also known her whole life, it was never this fun and comfortable.

Lucas stroked her hair away from her face, tucking a

strand behind her ear, his touch sending tingles dancing down her neck. "I'm glad Grady dropped out," he admitted.

"Well, he had to. I'm sure he didn't plan for his mother to get sick."

"No. But it's probably a good thing he left."

"What do you mean?"

"It would have been just as hard for him to play Mr. Darcy, always looking over his shoulder."

Aria frowned. "At what?"

Lucas gave her a sardonic look. "At me. Glaring at him from the sidelines."

"Would you have done that?"

Lucas shrugged, his fingers making gentle trails over her face, tracing her lips, flowing down her neck. "I would. And who knows, he might have met with some mysterious accident."

"I hope you're joking."

"I am. Of course." Lucas grew serious. "But I know the more time we spend with each other, the less I like the idea of anyone else being your Mr. Darcy. And I'm not even going to talk about the final kiss."

"It wouldn't be on the lips."

"I don't care if it was a chaste kiss on the back of your hand," Lucas said, growing serious. "I didn't like it."

"You're not getting all possessive now, are you?"

"I wasn't before."

She smiled at that. "No, you weren't."

"I didn't dare get that way. Not around your father."

"No, that was his schtick. With you."

Lucas grew quiet, tilting his head as if to see her from another angle. "I didn't see him as being possessive. More protective."

Aria thought back to the sermon on Sunday, filtering her own mixed emotions over her father.

"I suppose." She had to let it go. It was over; he was gone. "But let's talk about something more fun."

"More fun than running lines? I think we got most of them down. We should call it a night and head to the Pasta Place for dinner."

She didn't reply right away, unsure she wanted to be so public so soon with their still-fragile relationship.

Lucas caught the hesitation, his face holding a pained expression.

Then Aria set the script aside, stood, and took his hand in hers. "Why don't we? I'm buying. After all, once you pay me my share of the farm, I'll be rolling in the dough."

"Well, isn't that an interesting visual? Almost as interesting as me in a wet shirt."

Aria frowned a moment, then realized what he was saying. She smacked him on the arm. "You are incorrigible."

"And I even know what that means."

She laughed again, feeling a lightness she hadn't felt in a long time.

"THE PLACE fuller than I thought it would be." Lucas frowned as he looked around the restaurant.

"I'm sure we can find a spot." Aria stood beside him, fidgeting.

He sensed that she had been nervous about showing up in public with him.

Then she caught him by the arm. "Or we could go to the Grill and Chill."

"I'm kind of in a pizza frame of mind," Lucas said, shooting her a look of concern. She sounded tense. As he glanced around the restaurant, he saw Cole in one of the booths.

Looking directly at them and frowning.

Was he the reason she was so uptight?

He felt his back stiffen. He knew he wasn't Cole's favorite person even before he had broken up with Aria. Lucas didn't imagine that he had gained any points or status since then. In fact, while he had not admitted as much to Aria, he was surprised Cole was willing to sell him the land.

"But we can go if you want," he offered, lowering his voice.

Then, to his surprise, she shook her head and lifted her chin. "No, let's eat here. I don't want to support Gord."

"Why not?"

"Tell you later," she said, just as Stephanie approached them with menus in hand.

"For two?" she asked with the faintest hint of innuendo.

"That would be correct, Miss Bingley," he returned, shoving his hands in his pockets.

"Today I'm simply Stephanie Rauscher. Humble waitress." She may be a humble waitress, but her curious gaze flicked from him to Aria, and in that moment, he realized what they were up against.

That they would be the talk of the town within days, if not hours.

Stephanie led them to an empty table, thankfully toward the back of the restaurant. "This is usually reserved for your brother Liam and nephew Matthew," she noted as they slipped into the chairs. "But they and Aubrey are out on a date, too."

Lucas didn't bother to correct her. Was this a date? Or just two people who were hungry?

"I'll be back with some water, and you can tell me what you want to drink." Stephanie's curious gaze skittered over them, but Aria was studying the menu, as if she didn't know it by heart. Lucas knew she and her friends from the Breakfast Club had their meetings here most of the time. At least that's what he understood from Karissa, who often joined them. In fact, Aubrey opened the restaurant early just for them on Breakfast Club days.

"Busy in here," Lucas observed, thankful that his seat didn't face the main room so he couldn't catch Cole staring daggers into his back.

"I'm glad for Aubrey. It was a gamble for her to do all the work she did to get the restaurant back to profitability."

"No kidding. Especially considering she intended to sell it after she fixed it up."

"I'm glad she and Liam got back together again, and that she changed her mind." She gave him a careful smile.

"Me too. He's a lot happier than before. He and his ex-wife weren't a good fit." Liam didn't want to talk about his brother's love life.

But then he remembered something else she had said.

"Why don't you want to support Gord? At the Grill and Chill?"

Aria flushed a little, then gave him a shrug. "It's just a silly thing. Well, maybe not so silly." She fiddled with her napkin, unrolling it to take out the silverware. "It's Brooke."

"What about her?"

"She's had a crush on Gord for ages, but he doesn't seem to get the hint. I know some girls in the Breakfast Club tried to help him out there, but he's clueless. Brooke is such a sweetheart. I just wish she would respect herself a little more and realize how special she is. But that Gord can't see that… well…" Aria gave another shrug, her mouth twisted into an expression of displeasure.

"Remind me not to get on the wrong side of the Breakfast Club," he declared, but as soon as the words popped out of his mouth, he realized that he had already been there.

"We are a formidable bunch of women," she agreed.

Stephanie returned with their water.

"I'm ready to order," Aria told Stephanie, then glanced over at Lucas. "Do you need a few minutes yet?"

"Nope. I know what I want. The usual," he said to Stephanie

She nodded, then left and Aria quirked a sly look in his direction. "You have a usual that she remembers? How often do you come here?"

"Often enough. Believe it or not, even when it's busy here, it's quieter than at the house. Things can get kind of wild, especially now that the R's are in full pout mode."

"What about?"

Lucas held up his hand, ticking off the list on his fingers. "Community service, no driving, curfew, limited phone time. Burke and Karissa put the hammer down on them."

"That was because of the accident, right?"

"More because they lied about the accident. I feel bad sometimes for taking off on Burke and Karissa, so I'll often take Jacob with me, just to give him a break. He doesn't always say much, but I think he enjoys getting away from the R's when they're on the rampage."

"That's good of you."

"Maybe. Self-preservation has always run strong in me." He gave her a crooked grin to show he was teasing. "But noisy as it gets, it's still not as bad as when we were all younger, filling up the house with noise and fights and hassling. I still don't know how my parents did it."

"You always seemed like a happy family."

"We were, mostly, though, like I told you, we've had our issues. Mom and Dad had some rough spots."

"But they got through it."

"What about your parents? How did they get along? I didn't get to know your mother much."

She clenched her fork, and he wondered if he had strayed into a forbidden topic. Then she gave a light shrug, as if shunting off whatever might have bothered her. "Well, we were kind of sneaking around then," she said with a teasing smile, so no, you wouldn't have gotten to know her well."

"I do remember she laughed a lot."

"She did. Loved a good joke."

"I know it was devastating for your father when she died."

She just gave a tight nod of her head, and Lucas sensed she felt the same.

"I remember seeing him in the barn about three years after she died, sitting on a square bale of straw, just staring, jaw clenched. Like he was holding everything in. I snuck back out so he wouldn't see me. Broke my heart to see such grief."

Aria pressed her lips together, nodding in understanding. So much sorrow between them.

He fiddled with his fork, then looked across the table at her. "I never realized it, but you know, we're both orphans."

"That sounds so sad." She pressed her hand to her heart, as if to underline what he said. Then she looked like she was about to say something else when she looked past him, and her eyes went wide.

She angled sideways, as if to see better, then she grabbed Lucas' hand as he tried to turn to see where she was looking. "Not now," she hissed.

Lucas wanted to look just to be ornery, but why get on Aria's bad side on their first official outing? So, he stifled his curiosity over whatever was making her look so surprised and shocked, hoping she would fill him in.

"Okay. They're sitting down now," she whispered. "But don't look."

"If you don't tell me what's going on, I might," he returned with a joking smile.

"All in good time." She looked past his shoulder again, then tugged on his hand to pull him closer.

"So, Brooke just came in," she shared, her voice lowered.

"Okay, that's not so earth shattering." Lucas grinned at her surprise.

"With Grady Thompson."

Lucas frowned at that. "I thought he was helping his

mother?" Then his eyes narrowed. "Is he gonna try to get his part back in the play? Because I'll fight him for it. I will. Duel at dawn."

"Don't get so melodramatic. He's way too far behind on the script. Besides, that's not the point, you goof. Didn't you hear me? Brooke just walked in with Grady."

"And you walked in with me."

This netted him a sardonic look. "Yes. And I think we both know what that will start."

"A trend?"

"You're being impossible."

"Nope. Just being Lucas."

"Same thing." She gave his hand a shake, as if to bring him back to whatever point she wanted to make. Then leaned closer, her voice so quiet, he had to strain to hear. "Grady was asking me one night at play practice about Brooke. He told me he likes her, but she only seems interested in Gord."

"Which she is." Then something else dawned on him. "Was that the time you two were sitting on the stage, all close and intimate?"

"What craziness are you spouting?" She shot him a deep frown.

"Not craziness. You two looked like you were planning your wedding."

"Wow, you're going to go all the way there?" Her lips curved into a teasing smile. "Maybe we were."

"Maybe that's not funny."

She nodded. "Maybe it isn't, but you know you don't have to worry about Grady." Then she grew serious. "You don't, you know."

"Good to know." He squeezed her hand. "So, Grady was asking about Brooke?"

"He wanted to know if he had a chance with her. I told him to go for it."

"Good call. Maybe it won't hurt Gord to have a little competition."

"Maybe it wouldn't hurt Gord to get a life. He doesn't deserve Brooke's attention." The edge in Aria's voice made him smile, but also gave him the tiniest jitter.

"Do we ever deserve each other?" he asked.

"Probably not, but we can keep trying."

Warmth and familiarity filled him as their eyes met across the table. A shared recognition of the work that a relationship required.

I am doing it right this time, he promised himself. *I am doing the hard work.*

"Well, this will deflect the gossip off us," Lucas reasoned, sitting back, folding his arms over his chest.

"I would think so. Much bigger deal."

"Different. Ours…I think is a fairly large deal."

She chuckled at that, and then Stephanie brought their dinner. Two plates piled high with creamy pasta, bits of red peppers, and sausage poking through. All creating a sensory overload that made his stomach grumble and his mouth water.

"This looks amazing." He inhaled a deep draft of the tantalizing aroma and gave Stephanie a grin.

She gave him a coy smile back, then left.

"You have to stop doing that," Aria warned, picking up the cloth napkin beside her and spreading it out on her lap.

"Sniffing my food?"

"Well, that, and flirting with the waitress."

"What? That? That's not flirting. That's investing."

"In what?"

"Excellent service," he pronounced with a grin. But then he grew serious. "Trust me Aria, there isn't a woman in this restaurant, in this town, province, country etc. that can even come close to you."

Her eyes locked with his, and she slanted him a crooked

smile, lifting one corner of her mouth. He recognized the look. One that wanted to believe him but hesitated to commit.

"I know you've been told countless times how beautiful you are, and I'm not adding to those compliments, but I know you, I see you. Who you are behind the pretty and the fancy and the elegant." He was on the verge of telling her she held his heart, but something held him back. Something in the faint shadow he caught flit across her expression. She was holding something back yet, he sensed it.

But then her smile softened, and a faint flush colored her cheeks, and the uneasiness gripping him eased.

His stomach growled again, and it was time to eat. Just before he started, however, he laid his hand on the table between them, palm up. He wasn't sure if Aria would understand what he was trying to do, but to his pleasant surprise, she laid her hand in his. He curled his fingers around hers, squeezing gently as he bowed his head, praying a silent blessing over the food.

And also thanking God for this time he could spend with this incredible woman. He wasn't sure where things were going, but he laid everything in God's hands.

When he looked up, it was to see Aria smiling, her eyes bright. Then she ducked her head, picking up her fork.

"This looks so good. I'm glad you talked me into getting it," she said.

"Aubrey and her father make their own pasta, you know," he said. "Matthew keeps informing me of that factoid. He's a huge fan."

Aria nodded her acknowledgement, her mouth full. She lifted the napkin to her mouth and wiped her lips. "I remember coming here when Aubrey's mom was still around. Me and my friends would stop by after school, and Aubrey would be waiting on tables and…" She let the sentence trail off, then looked down, her cheeks once again flushed.

"Then what?" Liam urged.

"Not one of my best memories or moments." She chewed her lip, pushing her pasta around on her plate. "We weren't always the nicest to Aubrey. She had a lot to deal with. I'm just thankful she's been able to forgive me and the other girls who used to be so unkind to her."

"Honestly, I can't imagine you being unkind."

"There's a reason they call me the princess," Aria noted with a harsh laugh. "But I don't know if I want to tell you all my dark secrets yet."

Lucas chuckled at that. "You mean there's more?"

Aria held his gaze as her mouth turned down a bit. Her eyes seemed to go dark, the shadow he saw earlier returning. Then she shook her head. "One secret at a time." She gave him a grin, as if to show him she was teasing.

They were both quiet as they ate, but it was a comfortable silence.

After a while, though, he needed to ask her.

“Have you thought any more about my offer to take you dancing?"

She nodded, swirling her fork in her noodles. "I think that could be a lot of fun. As long as it doesn't interfere with play practice."

"Well, you'll just have to tell me which weekend works for you."

For just a moment, he felt trepidation clutching him, followed by a whisper of second thoughts.

But he was sitting with her in a very public restaurant, her brother probably watching them even now. There wasn't much secrecy in Aspen Valley. By being with her here, by her agreeing to come with him, they had already made a step toward a more serious relationship.

He tried to slow his thoughts down, but it was difficult. Especially when the woman who had taken up so much of them over the last three years now sat across from him, smiling.

As they ate, the talk became inconsequential. Comments about the play. Other members of the community. Politics didn't come up, nor did anything of major consequence. They were just two people catching up, comfortable with each other. It was a gift, and he knew it.

"This looks cozy." Cole's voice broke into their conversation.

Aria, seemingly startled, dropped her fork with a clatter. Lucas turned around, looking up at her brother. Cole didn't look too thrilled. So much for a congenial evening.

"Good to see you here," Lucas said, forcing a light tone into his voice. "Courtney and Fenna with you?"

Cole shook his head. "It's just me and Alastair."

Lucas was curious why he was having dinner with his business partner, but that was none of his concern.

Right now, his concern was the frown on Aria's face, and the way she was fidgeting with her napkin.

"So, have you heard anything from land titles?" Cole asked his sister.

Why would he ask her this in public? Didn't they talk to each other?

"I told you I'd let you know as soon as I heard anything." Aria glanced past him. "Is Alister pushing you?"

"I'd prefer not to talk about that in public."

At that, Aria lifted her chin. "You seem okay with asking other questions in public."

The challenging tone in her voice gave Lucas hope.

"You're right. I'm sorry." Cole's apology was a surprise. Cole was a good person, but he also had a lot of pride, which Lucas knew both from his brothers and from his own past dealings with the guy.

"Well, I better push on." Cole said, glancing from Aria over to Lucas. He held Lucas' eyes for a heartbeat longer than necessary, but Lucas picked up his cue from Aria and held Cole's gaze, keeping his expression neutral.

Then Cole gave Lucas a curt nod and walked away.

As he left, Lucas turned back to Aria, who was frowning at her brother's back, eyes narrowed.

"You okay?" Lucas asked.

Aria gave him a tight nod. "I am, but I need to have a little chat with my brother."

"What about?" As if Lucas didn't know. He had a strong suspicion that his name would be part of the conversation.

"That's between me and him." She gave him a quick smile. "Now, about that date we've got coming up. Let's figure out some details."

Chapter 11

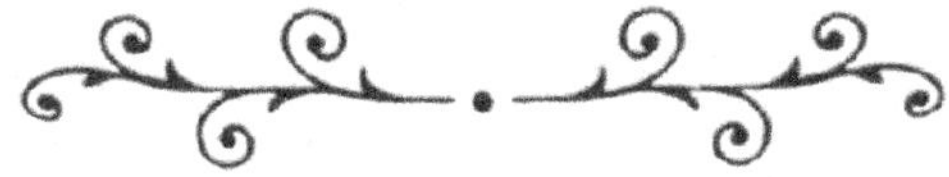

Aria brushed her hand over the shirt she wore. Too fancy? Not fancy enough? Would the plaid one be too on the nose?

Getting ready for a date had never made her this edgy before. She had even texted Brooke, asking how she should wear her hair.

To her surprise, Brooke didn't answer. Puzzling indeed. Brooke lived with her phone in her hand or in her back pocket. She was always available.

Consequently, Aria was on her own in the hair department. She pulled part of her hair back in a Dolly Partonesque half ponytail – a bit puffy, and yet all country. She wore gold hoop earrings, and the blue jeans were an obvious choice. She found the most comfortable ones she had. A simple shirt, tied at the front, draped over her glittery tank top. It would have to do.

Guys have it so easy, she thought, touching up her lipstick. A nice shirt, blue jeans, and they were ready for church, going out, just about anything. Even the auction mart, for goodness sakes.

If she had to go to the auction mart, she would need to go shopping for other clothes.

Then her doorbell rang, and she had no more time to make wardrobe changes.

She walked to the door, trying to slow her racing heart and quiet her second thoughts.

She opened the door, and Lucas stood there, weight resting on one leg, hand strung up in his pocket, cowboy hat pushed back on his still glistening hair.

His eyes widened. "Wow, you look amazing."

And all the dithering she had done, standing in front of her closet, was suddenly worth it.

"Why, you're not too hard on the eyes, either," Aria returned. "I might have to fight a few women off tonight."

"I was going to say the same thing. Except about guys."

"Maybe we better just stick together to avoid confrontations," Aria returned with a chuckle. "I'll just grab my purse and coat."

She was back in no time, and soon they were sitting in his truck, heading out of Aspen Valley. Lucas had country music playing on the radio, a soft counterpoint to the hum of tires on the pavement.

The ambience hearkened back to many a trip they had made in a much older truck, smelling of diesel and leather as they stole away from her farm, heading out to the swimming hole, the lookout point, a clandestine party.

Sneaking around, her father had accused her. Which is what they were doing, but the way he said it made it sound worse than it was.

Aria shook off the memory, laying her head back, turning to look at Lucas. It was still light out, but the lowering sun cast his face into interesting shadows. His cheeks and jaw shone from his recent grooming. Which was a little too bad. She kind of liked him looking stubbly, rough and ready.

Like a cowboy.

"What are you doing?" Lucas asked, shooting her a concerned glance.

She felt a momentary flush of self-consciousness, then brushed it away.

"Just staring," she admitted.

"That's what I thought you were doing."

"Does it make you feel uncomfortable?"

He shrugged, tapping his fingers on the steering wheel in time to the beat of the music. "Maybe a little. But the vain part of me kinda likes it."

"I'm sure that's not a new thing for you," she commented, try to keep her tone light. "Having a girl stare at you."

He caught one corner of his mouth between his teeth as he stared ahead at the road flowing past them. "There's been a few girls…"

"A few?"

"Yes. Nothing serious. Just a date here and there."

Aria held up a hand. "You don't need to tell me. Unless you want to."

"I'm not about to pour out my heart and all my confessions," he continued, his tone deep, quiet. "Trouble is, I lived such an itinerant lifestyle. And I was never one for temporary relationships. I had my eye on the prize."

She thought back to a few things he had said to her. About her father. Again, another coil of confusion. But she wanted everything out in the open between them. "Eye on the prize being…"

"Winning the NFR like your dad did. Twice."

"You hit it once," Aria returned.

His gaze shot to hers. "How do you know?"

"My father wasn't the only one watching your journey."

Lucas reached across the truck, taking her hand in his. "You know why I was gone, don't you? Why I left? You believe me, don't you?"

The intensity in his voice created a quiver of concern.

"I know, and I understand. But let's look ahead."

His hand tightened on hers, acknowledging her comment. "You're right. Like trying to remember how to do the Electric Slide?"

"Oh, that's an oldie, but goodie I haven't done in a long time," she returned. "Maybe you can teach me something new."

"I attended a few dances on the road, picked up a few ideas." He gave her a quick smile. "But nothing can beat an old-fashioned two-step."

"I have to say, that was one of our best ones."

"That and the waltz," he said.

She said nothing to that, knowing it was true. Though she had never gone out dancing with Drew, she had never wanted to. Country dancing was something she only shared with Lucas.

They learned all the steps they knew in his parents' living room: stereo blasting, Burke, Shelby, Liam, and Celeste spinning around and bumping into each other. Sometimes his parents would join in as well.

And sometimes they would practice on their own, in the hayloft of his parents' barn.

It was something she'd only ever done with him. She wanted to keep it special.

Now she was glad she had.

Lucas didn't pull his hand out of hers, and they drove the rest of the way in a companionable silence.

"ARE you sure your ankle can take this?" Lucas asked, taking Aria's hand in his, belatedly remembering her fall.

He had to raise his voice to be heard above the twang of the singer, the steady beat of drums, and the wailing of guitar. All around them, people were laughing and joking, glasses clinking. It was a long time since he had danced, but he was sure looking forward to spinning Aria around the floor.

Like Aria said, they always fit well together.

"Now isn't the time to ask," she called back, but she was grinning as she followed him. "But yes, I'm fine."

Lucas caught a few envious looks from the other guys. Not that he blamed them. Aria was easily the best-looking woman here, but he knew better than to mention that to her. He knew telling her she was pretty wasn't going to earn any points. Her smile was deeper, and her eyes sparkled brighter when he told her how accomplished she was. How smart she was, which was also true.

They found an empty spot on the floor. She turned to him. He caught her hand in one of his, dropped his other onto her waist as they waited for the beat. They took a few hesitant steps, then caught the rhythm. A few more, and then they were spinning and weaving over the floor.

A few turns and pivots, and she pulled away from him, spinning under his arm, her hair fanning out like a golden flame. Then back, another spin and another step away. It took nothing for them to drop into their old rhythms. A pass-through behind them, then around as they caught hands again.

"Haven't lost our touch," she called out, her grin as wide as his.

He saw sidelong glances from some of the other dancers. He knew they looked good together. His dark hair. Her blonde. Her trim figure, enhanced by snug blue jeans. How effortless they were with each other. Each anticipating what the other would do. Completely in sync.

How I have missed this, Lucas thought, pulling her just a little closer to him as they executed another spin on the balls of their feet. The song ended, but Aria kept her hand on his shoulder, waiting. A few people left the floor, but they stayed.

The band started up. Another two-step.

"Should we show these people how it's really done?" he asked, noticing they had a little more room. He gave her another little nudge that she acknowledged, then she spun away, catching his hand as they moved around each other, catching hands behind his back, a pass over their heads, facing each other, and then another spin.

The complicated moves came back so easily.

They were both laughing, smiling their enjoyment, caught up in the sheer joy of being together and dancing to the music.

The set ended, and he pulled her close for one more spin and a duck, which Aria played up, leaning back, her arms clasped around his neck as he bent over, her one leg coming up in a kick.

As they straightened, he pulled her close, her head tucked against his neck, as a few people clapped and hooted, whistling and cheering.

He didn't know if the flush on Aria's cheek was the result of embarrassment or exertion, but the sparkle in her eyes made the dramatic move worth every bit of attention. He held her close for a moment, then the lights dimmed, and the band struck up the first few bars of "Unchained Melody."

They waited a moment, as if each was mentally counting out the rhythm, and then as easily as they had slid into the two-step, they glided into the waltz. At first their movements were elegant, balanced, then their steps grew shorter, slower, and then they were hardly dancing at all, taking shuffling steps, his arms tight, holding her close as she laid her head on his shoulder. He bent his head over hers, inhaling the essence of her, the soft floral scent she always wore.

He had never felt so right, never felt like his world was complete until now. Dancing with the woman who had always held his heart in her delicate hands. Being together out in public.

Unashamed.

He couldn't help recalling the times when they had been so careful, watchful. As if she were embarrassed to be with him, even though she had protested when he mentioned that.

But now there were no constraints. No one judging.

All too soon the song ended, and when the last note died out, she leaned back, her hand resting on his shoulder, grinning up at him.

"You doing okay?" he asked.

"I'm a bit out of shape," she returned, her tone breathless. "And thirsty."

"Me too." He slipped his arm around her waist as they walked off the floor together.

"You guys were busting' some pretty awesome moves," one old cowboy called out as they sat at their table. Lucas just gave him a quick nod, then got up to get Aria her usual drink. Orange juice with a tiny splash of white wine.

He grabbed a beer and walked over to where she sat, setting her drink down in front of her.

"Unfortunately, no paper umbrellas," he said as he popped the top of his beer.

Aria lifted her glass and took a deep sip. "I might have to register a complaint with the management."

Lucas chuckled, taking her hand in his, wanting to maintain this connection between them.

They sat for a moment, glancing around. Lucas didn't recognize anybody in the room. Which made him dare to do the very next thing he did. His hand slid up her arm to her shoulder, and he shifted, leaning close, brushing a light kiss over her welcoming lips. Her hand came up to touch his cheek, then hold his jaw, as if to anchor him in place.

They sat in companionable silence for a few more songs, then Aria set her empty glass down, caught him by the hand, and pulled him to his feet for another round of dancing.

They danced and rested, danced and rested, the time flying past.

By eleven thirty, Lucas was fading. It had been a long day of hard work, and though he didn't want this magical evening to end, he had to be realistic.

"Is it almost pumpkin time?" Aria teased.

"Just about," he agreed, stifling a yawn. "Tomorrow Burke has got me riding fence on the back section, and I know I better show up all bright-eyed and bushy-tailed, or he's going to have questions." And he wasn't ready for those. He wanted to keep the memory of this evening to himself. To guard it and hold it close.

"I'll have to get to the office, too." Aria returned, flipping her hair back and hooking her purse around her arm.

"What's your afternoon looking like?" he asked as he caught her free hand, and they walked out the door together.

"More of the same."

"You work too hard."

"That's considered a compliment in legal circles," she laughed.

"And in Aspen Valley, to be honest," he noted as they stepped out into the fresh evening air.

They were halfway to his truck when she halted, her hand catching his arm.

"I almost forgot. I checked in with Land Titles. They hope to have the transfer by next week."

It was a testament to what a wonderful time they'd had together that this news, which they had been waiting for, didn't even affect him as much as being beside Aria did. Spending a delightful and fun evening with her.

"You don't look especially excited."

He rested his hands on her hips, holding her eyes. "Honestly, that's good news and I am happy, but being with you makes me a lot happier."

"That's a stellar line." Aria grinned up at him. "How long did it take you to come up with it?"

"About thirty-two seconds," Lucas returned. "You inspire me to eloquent heights of prose."

She grew serious, then slid her hands to his shoulders, raised herself up on tiptoe, and pressed a quick kiss to his lips. Then another.

"I'm glad you feel like that, because being with you makes me happy, too."

He leaned back against his truck, pulling her close to him, dragging out the moment. Once they got inside his truck, heading back to Aspen Valley, he felt as if the memories the town created would dilute the magic.

So, he stayed where he was, kissing her again as she leaned into him, her arms twined behind his neck.

Lucas brushed a strand of hair away from her face, tucking it behind her ear, letting his finger trace a gentle line down to her neck then up to her chin as he cupped her face, his thumb making imperceptible circles over her cheek.

He wasn't sure what to say, unwilling to break the moment by using the wrong words.

Much as he wanted to, he wasn't ready to tell her how he felt. How quickly he had fallen for her again.

It was confusing. They had a previous relationship, a shared history. It should be easy to let her know how he felt.

Yet neither of them was the same person as they had been back then. Life had chiseled parts away, toughened others. And despite the confidence he'd gained by competing, he wondered if he could begin to measure up to her father.

"Aria, I feel like I need to tell you –"

But Aria stopped him, pressing her finger lightly against his lips.

"We're right here, right now. Let's not go beyond that."

It was something he used to say to her, when she wasn't sure of herself or worried about what her father would say if he found out.

At the thought of Steven, Lucas couldn't stop a small shiver of foreboding.

What would he think right now? Would he still think Lucas wasn't the right person for his daughter?

What about you? Do you think you're the right person for her?

"It's just you and me right now," she continued, as if she knew what he was thinking. "Let's just see where life takes us."

He smiled at that and gently drew her close against him, giving her one last hug.

Then reluctantly, he straightened, took a step away, and fished his keys out of the back pocket of his pants. He spun the key ring around his finger, which elicited another smile from Aria. How often had he done that before? A shared signal that it was time to go.

The drive back was quiet. He kept the music low, glancing over at her, catching her doing the same.

Smiling when their eyes connected.

An hour later, he pulled up to her apartment. He put the truck in park and got out, but before he could open the door for Aria, she was already standing on the sidewalk, slamming the door behind her. The sound was like a note of finality echoing through the night.

Lucas dropped his arm across her shoulder as he walked her to the door. He looked up at the apartment, frowning.

"What's on your mind?" Aria asked.

"I guess I'm wondering why you are living in this apartment when you've got a perfectly good house on your dad's place to live in."

Aria bit her lip, and he wondered if he was being insensitive. Maybe it hurt her too much to be in her family's home by herself?

"Never mind. Don't answer that," he said. "I'm sure the farm has some hard memories for you. I'm sure you're still grieving your father. Maybe even your mother."

Aria gave a tight nod. "Yes. Hard memories, for sure."

"If it's any consolation, I have them too. I think about your dad a lot, and I'm glad that I at least made it to the NFR rodeo, even if I didn't get as high up the rankings as he did."

"You don't need to compare yourself to my father. You are your own person." Aria planted a hand on his chest, her fingers curling against his shirt. Her voice held a note of determination. "You don't have to be what anyone else wants you to be. You are a good, kind man in your own right. Don't compare yourself to anybody."

The harsh note in her voice created another shiver of uncertainty for him. Before he could ask her more, she gave him a smile, opened the door, and stepped into her apartment's foyer. She swiped her fob, and as the entrance door slid open, she caught it, gave a quick glance back over her shoulder, accompanied by a waggle of her fingers, and then she was inside, striding to the stairs.

Lucas stood there a moment, trying to absorb her last comment. Trying to parse the emotions braided through the words.

He gave his head a shake. He knew she didn't enjoy talking about her father. He thought it was because she missed him, but something in her voice produced a disjointed feeling that didn't fit with the notion of grieving for her father.

He shook off the premonition. He was just tired, and maybe it was his optimistic thoughts that made him think she didn't worship her father as much as he thought she did. Maybe he wanted that to happen, so he wouldn't feel like he couldn't measure up.

He strode to his truck, but just before he got in, he glanced up at the windows of Aria's apartment, lit up now. He saw her in the window, her arms folded over her stomach as she looked down at him. She gave him another little wave, which he returned. He climbed into his truck and drove away, his thoughts chasing him as he drove.

Chapter 12

"This is the last scene of the play," Courtney announced. "We're doing a rough read of this, and then we're done for the night.

"And then what?" Lucas asked, happy they were quitting early. He was still tired from his late night on Friday with Aria, then working all day Saturday.

"Then we go back to the beginning again. Run straight through it a bunch more times. And then a few dress rehearsals."

Brooke groaned, and Courtney shot her a frown. "You have the clothes ready, don't you?"

"We're not opening for at least another month."

"That month will slip by quicker than you think."

"I guess." Brooke sighed as she tucked a strand of hair behind her ear, glancing over at Grady. Because he had seen them together the other night, Lucas thought for sure that he would see more evidence of a relationship between them.

But both had kept their distance from each other all evening.

"All right, people, take your places. Mr. Darcy, Miss Bennett, I'm sure you're very much looking forward to this scene." Courtney gave Lucas an arch look, but he didn't rise to the bait. Aria's expression was as impassive as his.

He didn't need anyone to know that kissing Aria was nothing new for either of them.

"I want you to start from the part where she discovers what he's done to help her hapless sister, and then do the lines of the play from there. And then he gives her a very chaste kiss. Emphasis on 'chaste.'"

They worked their way through the scene until they came to the last page.

Aria's hand rested on Lucas' shoulder, and her eyes glimmered.

"I know you can do better than a chaste kiss," she whispered, her tone taunting.

"Do you really want to go there?" He winked at her, tugging her ever closer to him. But she sensed what he was about to do and stepped back.

"Mr. Darcy, I think you are being rather presumptuous," she teased, wagging an admonishing finger at him, even as her eyes twinkled.

"Thou makest it to be so," Lucas returned. "But I thinkest thou is the presumptuous one."

"When we're venturing into Shakespearean language, might be time to call it a night." Courtney sat on the stage, blowing out a sigh as she arched her back. For a moment, Lucas felt sorry for her, and he wondered if she might have taken on too much.

"Coffee's on if anyone is interested," Karissa called out. "Aubrey sent some cookies along."

"Did you want anything?" he asked Aria as people moved to the table.

"Sorry," Aria apologized, shoving her script into her purse and slinging it over her shoulder. "I have a deposition to prepare for tomorrow, and I'm behind on all my other stuff."

"You might need to hire another lawyer," Cole suggested,

munching on a cookie as he joined them. He held one out to Lucas, who shook his head. “You’ve been pretty busy lately.”

“I’ve got Freya. She covers most of the other stuff.”

“She can’t do it all. I know Cody’s been complaining about how much time she spends at your office.”

“If Cody has a problem, he and Freya have to figure that out themselves,” Aria asserted with a shrug.

“I think you’re just too much of a control freak to hand even one rein over to someone else.”

"I am what I am," she returned. “And I am tired, so I’m leaving.”

Cole seemed to take the hint, glanced over at Lucas, then left before she did.

Lucas tried not to read anything into the look her brother gave him. What was happening between Lucas and Aria shouldn’t be Cole’s concern. But despite his self-talk, the specter of Aria and Cole’s father still lurked in the shadows.

Along with his expectations for his daughter.

Aria gave Lucas a secretive smile, and a shiver danced down his back. He knew everyone’s eyes were on him, but he didn’t care.

He followed her out of the hall.

"I’m guessing that look was a hint for me to come outside as well?” he teased, their feet crunching on the graveled parking lot.

"I just need a kiss from you to hold me through until our next play practice.”

“But that’s not until day after tomorrow,” he said, walking through the star-spangled night to her car.

“Sorry. I’m just too busy between now and then.”

“I think Cole is right. You should hire someone else.”

“I know. I just don’t feel like going through the vetting process.”

“Well, you know I can’t believe I’m about to say what I’m about to say.”

"That's not convoluted at all," Aria teased, opening her car door and tossing her purse inside. But she closed it and turned to him, leaning back against her vehicle.

"Why don't you hire Drew?"

Surprise trickled over her face. "My old boyfriend?"

Lucas shrugged away her question. "Well, you said you were just friends."

"Yes. We were and are."

"So, maybe he wants to move back to Aspen Valley, too. I heard from his sister, Jewel, that he's not too thrilled with the ridiculous hours he's been putting in where he's working. And he's tired of the city." He moved closer, pulling Aria into his arms, but holding her so he could still lose himself in her gorgeous eyes.

"Since when are you talking to Jewel Rozak?" She tapped her finger on his shoulder in a reprimanding gesture. "Should I be jealous now?"

"As if." He chuckled, brushing a kiss over her forehead, then her cheek. He tried to capture her lips, but she pulled back, her hand on his chest.

"As if what?" Her voice held an arch tone, and he knew what she was angling for.

"I only have eyes for you, Miss Bennet. From the moment I saw you –"

"We first met when I was five."

"I've only had eyes for you. Remember that Valentine card I gave you?"

She ran her finger down the opening of his shirt, smiling. "I still have it."

"Really?"

"Yes, really."

"That makes my heart happy that you're still my Valentine." He twirled a strand of her hair around his finger, then released it, tucking it behind her ear. Simple things, small connections, what once would have been invasions of personal space were now tranquil forays toward a deeper intimacy.

"Are we still on for that movie Friday night?" he murmured, distracted by the shine of her lips. Wanting to kiss her and yet enjoying this quiet, teasing conversation.

Ordinary times. What he had missed with any of the girls he dated. This high level of comfort.

"Not sure action adventure is my genre, but if it means sitting beside you eating popcorn in a dark theater, I think I can force myself to watch explosions and chases for a couple hours."

"You can always close your eyes," Lucas offered, trailing a finger down her cheek, then curling it under her chin.

It was all the invitation she needed. She wrapped her arms around his neck, and their lips met in a long, soft, gentle kiss. They stood there for a while, and Lucas reluctantly pulled away.

"I know this might be soon," he said, feeling his way around this conversation he'd been wanting to have with her ever since their dance. Ever since he felt the sense of complete and utter rightness of being with her.

"What are you trying to say?"

Her guarded expression almost made him back off. But he knew what they shared was real and true, and that pushed him forward.

"I have a feeling you know what's happening between us. I believe you know how I feel, and I'm thinking you're on the same page. But we're not teenagers anymore, trying to figure out our lives and relationships. We've both been through difficult times. I think we both know what we want. At least I know what I'd like to see happen with you and me."

She held his gaze, assessing him. Then she pulled back. "I know what I want, too. But there's a few things I need to sort out first."

Her words were spoken quietly, but he felt a weight behind

them. He wanted to ask what they were but sensed she wouldn't tell him.

She didn't push you away, so take it one step at a time.

Or one pause at a time.

"I understand. I do, but you also need to know, nothing will make me change my mind about us. I know I don't deserve you, like your father said, but I'd like to think that he would appreciate who I am now."

He knew that mentioning her father would create a small retreat, but he also hoped that by introducing him slowly into their conversations, she would get over the grief she obviously still carried over his death.

She nodded, then looked away as he thought she might.

"I'll see you the day after tomorrow," was all she replied. Then, without another look his way, she got into her car and left.

But before she had ducked into the car, he caught the shimmer of tears.

It broke his heart, but he also knew, from his own grief, that with time it would ease.

He hoped he could be with her to help her through it.

"ENOUGH EXPLOSIONS FOR YOU?" Lucas teased as they walked together through the cool evening air.

He wasn't ready to end the evening, so he headed toward the Grill and Chill. Gord always left the cafe open two hours later on movie nights.

"I don't know. Looked kind of CGI to me." Aria tucked her arm inside Lucas' as they walked, and he pressed her arm closer to his side.

They had spent the past two hours snuggled up against each other, but it still didn't seem like they had spent enough time together.

Thankfully, Aria didn't seem keen on going home either. At least, he assumed that from the way she didn't even slow down as they passed his truck.

"You think so? Based on your extensive pyrotechnic experience?"

"I almost burned down the back pasture once when I wanted to have a marshmallow roast with my friends. And when I was younger, I lit a fire outside the tack shed. So, I know a few things about fire."

"You lit a fire in the tack shed? Your dad's sacred space? With his favorite custom-built saddle inside?"

"And mine and Cole's," she added.

"How did I not know about this rebellion?" Lucas asked, sounding mock horrified.

"No one knew. As soon as I got it started, it took off much quicker than I thought it would. I freaked out and stomped it out, then poured water all over it. Then I cleared out all the evidence. I buried my clothes with the evidence, hosed myself off with ice cold water, and snuck into the house to put on other shirt and pants. Thank goodness the door to the shed was closed, so the smoke smell wouldn't go outside. But I got up in the middle of the night to make sure."

Lucas pulled back, turning her to look at him.

"My, my. Such planning. I'm not so certain you aren't a closet pyromaniac."

Aria chuckled at that, tugging him along down the street. "That is an oxymoron. Pyromaniacs don't hang out in closets. They'd burn them down."

"True enough," Lucas agreed. "Now that we're sharing secrets, do you have any more you think I should know?"

"Why do you want to know?" Aria gave his arm a jiggle, smiled up at him, her tone coy, her lips inviting.

Lucas didn't want coffee at the Grill and Chill anymore. He glanced down the street toward the path leading to the lake, then followed it.

The lamps lining the boardwalk and the beach area gave just enough light to show where they were going, but they were not so bright that he felt exposed.

He walked to the nearest bench, sat down, and pulled her down beside him.

He knew where things were going. In a few days, he would be signing off on a land deal that would tie him to Aspen Valley for the rest of his life.

And he knew he wanted Aria at his side.

Despite that determination, however, he still felt that a shadow hung between them. He couldn't put his finger on it. A hesitation on Aria's part. A retreat whenever he inched toward talk of the future.

He was content, for now, to let things drift along, knowing that each kiss, each moment together moved them closer to his eventual goal.

Aria leaned back onto the bench, her arms crossed as she looked out over the lake. The road that snaked around it was partially hidden by trees, but the lights of the cars driving along it glittered through the foliage.

The moon hung above them, a curved crescent, looking like it was hooked onto the stars that glittered above.

Waves swished onto the shoreline ahead of them, creating a soft counterpoint to the sound of traffic behind them.

When Lucas settled down onto the bench beside her, he slipped his arm around her, pulling her close. She laid her head on his shoulder.

For a while they said nothing, each content with this tender moment of attachment.

Aria rested her hand on his leg, and he covered it with his own.

Though she was physically beside him, he sensed a growing reticence about her. He wasn't sure how to broach it, so he went with humor.

"You're so quiet. You must be thinking about the movie."

"I hate to burst your bubble, but it wasn't that memorable."

He chuckled at that. "Weren't you entertained?"

"Oh yes, I was."

He pushed on. "Why do I get the idea you have something on your mind? If it's not the movie, then what is it?"

She didn't reply right away, her fingers curling around his, squeezing lightly.

He knew enough to keep quiet, to wait for her.

"I have to leave on Sunday, so I won't be in church."

"You're worried about your spiritual well-being?"

She chuckled at that. "No. I've made a sudden last-minute decision and am going to go to Calgary. To talk to Drew Rozak."

"That is sudden."

"I don't know who talked to him, but he called me at work this morning, asking me if I was looking for a partner. In the business," she hastily added. "I had to go to Calgary anyway to meet with another lawyer on a case I'm working on, so I thought I would combine the two. He could only get away for the Sunday, so he's flying out, and we'll meet that day."

"Okay. That's…unexpected."

She frowned at him. "Why? You're said I should hire him to lessen my workload."

"No, you're right. It's just, it came up fast."

"I know. But I have a good feeling about this." She gave him a coy look. "And I wouldn't mind having more free time to spend with…someone special."

"I sure hope that 'someone special' is me," he teased.

In answer, she gave him a quick kiss.

"You know it," she whispered, resting her head back on his shoulder.

They sat a moment, and then suddenly she requested, "Tell me about my father. About your relationship with him."

This was unexpected.

"What you want to know?"

Another beat of silence. Then she shifted her head just enough to look up at him. "You got along with him well. I saw you two together. Saw you laugh together. I've always wondered what it was about you that created that connection with him?"

"I'm not sure. I think it was a combined love of rodeo and horses. And he always told me I reminded of him when he was younger." Lucas laid his cheek against her head, his thumb stroking her fingers. "When I first came back to town, you didn't want to talk much about your father. Why was that?"

Aria emitted a short laugh. "Part of it was because I missed him. And part of it was…" She fell silent. He wanted to prompt her to finish her sentence, but waited. "What things did you and my dad talk about?" she asked instead.

He decided to follow along.

"Horses. Horse training. How to ride a bucking bronco." His mind ticked back to those times in the arena with her father. Though he'd had a good relationship with his own father, somehow being with Steven Waldren had been different. They'd shared the same interests. And thankfully, his father had never seemed to mind the times he spent at the Waldren Ranch. In fact, at times, he'd encouraged the relationship, saying it was important to have a variety of adults in one's life. Lucas was thankful for his father's generosity in that department. Some fathers might have felt jealous.

"I got to hear a lot of stories about his time in the rodeo. He had a ton of experience."

"He did like being on the road."

"I know. And he often said that he regretted being gone so often." Lucas continued. "But he was thankful that he had the support he did from your mother. He missed her. A lot."

"So did we." Aria pulled away at that, leaning forward, her arms folded, resting on her knees, looking out over the water. Her voice held a note of sorrow, and Lucas rubbed her back lightly. Another small connection. Then she sighed, shooting him a quick glance over her shoulder. "What else did you talk about?"

"We talked about you guys," Lucas continued, sensing she wanted to hear more. "Mostly you. I know he loved you dearly. I know he struggled with his relationship with Cole."

She met this with silence and a slight stiffening of her back, but he carried on.

"I remember him talking about buying you your first horse. How he consulted with so many trainers on which was the best breed and temperament."

He was pleased to see her smile at that. "Well, he got me a good one," she recalled. "I rode Blossom until she got too old. She was the best horse I ever had. I put a lot of miles on her."

"I know your father enjoyed your rides together."

"I did too. For the most part."

"That was part of the problem for me. I saw all the things he gave you. I know how he cared for you. So, when he told me I wasn't worthy, I believed him."

"Do you still?"

"I still think I'm not worthy, but I also think that's up to you to decide. Not anyone else."

"Good to know," she teased, her smile glimmering into his soul. Then she grew serious again. "So, what else did you two talk about?"

"How he got into rodeo. How it was an escape for him."

"From what?"

"His father. He told me stories about growing up with his dad. I… I don't think he had an easy time of it."

Aria shot him a startled glance, her eyes glinting in the glow of the streetlights behind them. "He talked to you about his childhood?"

"You sound surprised."

Aria nodded. "He never talked much about his family. All

I knew was that he inherited the ranch from his father, who also inherited the ranch from my great grandfather. The Waldrens have been around here for a few generations. I know some stories, but the only thing my dad told me was that when he was young, his mother left his father. I never met her. I have some indefinite memories of my grandfather. None too positive. He was a grumpy old man. What did my dad say about him?"

"I remember him saying how difficult it was to be an only child. That his father demanded a lot from him." Lucas bit his lip, wondering if he should say anything more. But then, this was Aria he was talking to. A woman who was important to him. And though her father might not have said much to her about his upbringing, he was gone now. What would it hurt to let her know? "He never said anything to you about it?" he continued.

"Like I said, the only thing I ever heard him say about his father was that he had high expectations. The same expectations he seemed to have of me and, even more, Cole."

The note of bitterness in her voice pained him. "He was the same with me, if it's any comfort. But I think he was also the same way with himself. Nothing he did was ever good enough. He was never satisfied. Though he made it all the way to the NFR, he was always telling me he should have done better. Told me about all the mistakes he made."

"Funny that you got to be the recipient of those confidences."

Again, that harsh tone, which created a quiver of guilt.

He had to let go of that. He hadn't asked Steven for the things he had confided in Lucas.

"I'm getting the feeling there's more to the story?" Aria asked, obviously wanting to know more.

Lucas hesitated, trying to find the right way to tell her, but then went for direct. "He told me he hated his father. Apparently, his father abused him. Physically and emotionally."

Aria stared at him, frowning. "He said that? And you believed him?"

Lucas wasn't sure how to respond, feeling as if he was treading a very thin line and unsure of the boundaries of the conversation and where it would lead.

"He showed me the scars on his arm from where his father beat him when he was a kid." He wanted to ask if she'd ever seen them, but wasn't sure it was appropriate. "He also said his dad had pushed him off the hayloft. Broke his leg in two places. He told me that his father had a horrible temper. Steven suspected that was why he was divorced. But your dad stayed on the ranch because his mother didn't want custody of him. He told me that was hard on him. That's why he was so thankful for his marriage to your mother. Told me how much he loved her, and how heartbroken he was after she died. And how hard he grieved. I'm sure you must have read something about their relationship in those letters you got?"

Aria sucked in a quick breath, then stood and walked toward the water, her arms wrapped tightly around her midsection, head lowered. Lucas stayed where he was, not sure if he should follow. Not sure what to offer her.

She walked toward the edge of the water, standing silently, staring ahead. Then she bent her head, covering her face with her hands.

When he joined her, he saw anguish distorting her features.

"Why didn't you tell me?" Her accusation was an icy knife to his heart.

"He asked me not to. He said he didn't want to talk about it with you and Cole."

She dropped her hands to her side, staring at him as if she didn't know him. "And that was more important to you than letting me know this vital information about my father's life? It would have explained so much."

Again, Lucas felt as if the ground beneath him was shaky, his next steps unsure.

"I'm sorry if you thought I should have told you." He wanted to reach out to her, to reconnect, but kept his distance, waiting for her to make the first move. "I thought you knew."

"I dislike apologies that have qualifications attached," she snapped, sounding more like an attorney than a girlfriend.

Lucas felt the conversation slipping away from him in a direction he hadn't foreseen.

"Okay. You're right. I'm sorry. I should have said something." He hoped that eased her obviously ruffled feathers.

Aria shook her head. "You realize I need time to think about this."

He sensed she had no idea about the struggles of her father's childhood. She had looked and sounded surprised. Shocked.

And confused.

Should he have said anything at all? Because as she took another small step away from him, he felt as if he might lose her again.

"Why don't I take you home?" was all he could manage.

She nodded tightly and strode away from him to the truck, Lucas trailing in her wake.

Praying that all she needed was time to process this information instead of thinking he had betrayed her somehow.

Chapter 13

Aria looked over the yard of the ranch, her mind a tangle of thoughts and confusion. She'd been standing here for a long time, waiting for Cole, sifting through her last conversation with Lucas. He had texted her last night asking her if she was okay, apologizing again.

Even as she nursed her anger with him, part of her realized it wasn't his fault that her father hadn't told her or Cole. So, she had told him everything was fine, even though it wasn't entirely true.

Despite all her self-talk, sleep had eluded her. What Lucas told her spun through her thoughts, coloring her memories. If her thoughts had been confused before, they were now a snarl.

She asked Lucas for some time to process the information he'd shared, which included coming here to settle her troubled thoughts.

And talking to Cole.

She walked over to the house and onto the verandah, sifting and sorting through her memories.

Times she and her dad would sit on the porch and talk about what she wanted to do. Times he would say how proud he was of her. How he would smile and give her one of his quick side-arm hugs. How excited he was when he gave her Blossom, her princess bed, that shiny new car.

But juxtaposed against that were the times she would hear that same man outside, yelling at Cole, his fury creating genuine fear. How she would try to intervene, only to be yelled at and told to leave.

But then he would come into the house, smile at her, and she felt a mixture of guilty relief that she wasn't on the receiving end of her father's anger.

Cole had never told her the extent of their father's abuse until his funeral, when she had caught him in the basement of the church, crying and angry at the same time. They had talked later that night.

Cole's stories introduced a confusion about her father she was unsure where to place.

Listening to Lucas talk in such glowing terms about his relationship with Steven Waldren added another layer of perplexity. She knew Lucas wasn't exaggerating. She had seen how her father treated Lucas when he came around, which had made Cole's stories more bewildering.

And then those letters her father had written to her mother. Where to put that?

Which one of these men was her father?

She sat down on one of the Adirondack chairs on the porch, running her hand over the peeling paint, remembering helping her father build them. He'd spent a lot of time in his workshop after their mother had died. Cole stayed away, but she would come and hand her father nails and give suggestions.

Was losing his wife, their mother, what had triggered her father's temper? Was it grief? Repressed memories of his own father?

Her heart twitched as she tried to find her balance on the shifting ground of her memories.

She laid her head back on the chair, closing her eyes,

sending up a formless prayer for strength. For truth.

After what Lucas had told her, she texted Cole and asked him to meet her here. It was more private than her office, and it seemed fitting. They needed to talk.

But now it had been almost an hour since the time she had asked him to come. Maybe he'd had an emergency, but she was sure he would have texted or called if that was the case.

She pulled out her phone, wondering if she should text him. If she should just give up and leave.

But just as she was about to call him, she heard a vehicle entering the yard.

A truck drove up, stopped, and the engine was shut off.

Then Cole got out. He stood beside his vehicle for a while, and she knew he was casting over his own memories.

She felt a pang, knowing his were far different from hers.

Then he turned, saw her, and waved. The smile on his face kindled reluctant hope.

"Hey. Almost didn't notice you there," he said as he strode up the stairs, his footsteps echoing on the wood. "Sorry I'm late. You been here long?"

"I've been enjoying the peace. Work has been nuts."

"So, what did you want to talk about?" he asked, frowning now. "And why here?"

His frustration was like a searing ache. She stifled the urge to jump up and leave, instead, rubbing her palms down her pants, holding her ground.

"I thought it was appropriate."

Cole's features were set in a hard line, and for a moment, she thought he would leave. But then he gave a quick nod and dropped into the empty chair beside her.

"Lots of memories here," Aria commented, leaning back in her chair, trying to find the right opening for what she had to tell her brother.

"Yeah. Not always so good."

Aria heard the bitterness in his voice and, once again,

confusion buckled through her.

"I know, and I'm sorry about that."

Cole leaned back, his hands resting on the arms of the chair, his fingers tapping out an unconscious rhythm. Something he often did when he was uptight or nervous.

"I know you have different memories." Cole shot her a quick sidelong glance. "For some reason, Dad favored you."

"I wish I could have changed all that." Again, nothing more that she could add.

"Not your fault. You didn't ask for that any more than I asked for how he treated me."

Another pause. Another prayer for the right words to say.

"Did you have a chance to read those letters?"

After she had gone through them, she'd passed them to Courtney, who gave them to Cole. As she'd read the outpouring of love from her father to her mother, she had seen another side of him that wedged between her own memories.

He shook his head. "No. Truly haven't had time." Then he slanted her a wry look. "Besides, can't say I'm too interested. I doubt it would change anything."

Frustration nipped at her, but she couldn't fault him for wanting to keep all things about Steven Waldren at arm's length.

But she pressed on, wondering, hoping. "I was talking to Lucas yesterday. He told me something...." she paused. Something. Such a small word for this large piece of information. "Something that might explain a few things," she continued.

"What can you tell me that could make a difference?" The bitterness in Cole's voice wasn't encouraging. And yet, even as it registered, she wondered if there weren't times Cole struggled with an ambivalence about their father as well. She knew they'd had some good times together, even after their mother died. Horseback rides into the hills cradling Aspen Lake. Games they would play around the table.

"Do you remember Dad ever talking about his own father?" she asked.

Cole frowned, but kept his gaze on the yard. "No, never."

"Do you remember him much? Our grandfather?"

This elicited another shrug. "A few things here and there. I remember he was always grumpy. I remember complaining to Mom about him, and she said that Dad was dealing with his own pain. Didn't mean much to me then, though there were times I wondered what she meant."

This was new to Aria as well. Something else to fold into the backstory of their life.

"Why do you ask?" he continued.

Aria hesitated, but only for a few heartbeats. She felt a sense of inevitability surge through her. One way or the other, this conversation was happening. May as well get it done now.

"Lucas was telling me some memories Dad shared with him. About his own father, our grandfather."

"And?" Again, that clipped note of impatience.

"Apparently Grandpa treated Dad even worse than Dad treated you. Dad had a couple of scars on both his arms from him. He'd broken his leg in two places."

Cole's hands clenched the armrests of the chair, his knuckles turning white. "Does that justify Dad abusing me?"

"I'm not trying to justify his behavior at all. I'm just trying to show that maybe there's a reason for how he acted."

"You can't seriously think I should just say, 'oh, poor Dad.'" Cole leaned back, his arms pressed across his middle, lips tight, eyes narrowed. "He was abused, so he decided to pass that legacy on? He made a choice. I certainly don't abuse Fenna because I was."

His body language screamed censure and disapproval, and Aria regretted having this conversation. Wished she would have waited.

For what?

She leaned forward, trying to catch his eye as Cole blew out a harsh breath.

"I'm trying to understand him better," Aria explained. "Trying to sort out how I feel about him as well."

She waited, watching as Cole tapped his fingers against his arm, glaring ahead.

She drew on her experiences as a lawyer, letting the silence settle and do its work.

Cole fidgeted, sighed again, then, finally, lowered his arms. "Why do you to understand him? What difference will it make?"

"I guess it's because Lucas has different memories than I do than you do. So, who was Dad? Which person?"

"Again, why does that matter? It's in the past. Leave it be."

"Maybe, but I know the past seeps into the present, and I feel like it still affects you. I think Lucas and I are growing more serious, and I just feel like Dad looms above us all. And I don't want him to."

Birds sang into the quiet that followed. A faint breeze swished through the trees tucked up against the house. The faint hum of a diesel truck from the highway a few kilometers away floated past them.

Aria prayed while she leaned back into her chair, wondering what to say.

"He was so angry with me, so often," Cole finally shared. "And I never saw the same anger with you."

"I know that. I saw flashes of his temper, but I know they were not the same as what you dealt with."

Another sigh as Cole dropped his head back against his chair. "I hated him for so long…"

"Do you still?"

A shrug, another shiver of silence.

"I don't want to feel anything for him," he finally admitted. The faint break in her brother's voice shocked her.

And gave her a glimmer of hope.

"Do you think you might ever forgive him?" The question came from nowhere, but as soon as it was released, she felt as if it needed to be asked.

"Why? What would that do?"

Aria raked through her thoughts for the right thing to say.

"I think it might free you from anger." She kept her voice quiet, gentle, knowing she was treading into fraught territory. "It might free you from the hold I think he still has on you."

She waited for a response.

He pressed his hands against the chair and almost launched himself free. Then he turned to her, unbuttoned his shirt, pulled it off and turned his back to her. "You talked about the scars on our dad's arms. Do you see this?"

Aria couldn't stifle her gasp of shock at the ridged scar on his shoulder. "No broken bones, just a rip in my skin from when he hit me with a board that had a nail in it. He said he didn't know about the nail, as if that excused him hitting me in the first place." He pulled his shirt back over his shoulders, then rolled up a shirt sleeve, exposing another scar. "And only one of these, unfortunately, and only on one arm. Nothing like the couple you said Dad suffered, at least according to Lucas. But, you know, pretty impactful nonetheless." his voice was so cold, so hard, laced with scorn and pain.

Her stomach roiled at the sight.

"When…how…" She couldn't wrap her head around what she was seeing. All this time she had thought her father's treatment of Cole only involved verbal anger, which was bad enough.

But to see this?

"When? A few times. One night when I came back too late from a party, and he confronted me on the yard. Once when I didn't close the gate, and the horses got into Nate Montane's pasture. This happened in high school while he was buying you all those fun gifts. The horse, the saddle, the clothes. The car."

He spat the last words out, and she squirmed, withering guilt clenching her gut.

He buttoned up his shirt, his movements jerky, avoiding her gaze.

"Let me know when the title is transferred," was all he said before she could, once again, apologize for something she hadn't done. "Then I can move on from all of this." He waved his hand at the house behind him.

As he strode down the yard, desolation crowded her thoughts.

Because if things between her and Lucas went the way she thought they would go, they would live in this house. On this property.

How could Aria do that, knowing what had happened to her dear, beloved brother here?

LUCAS PULLED up to the mobile home Courtney, Cole, and Fenna lived in, fighting down a coiling uncertainty.

He wished Aria was here with him, but also he knew he had to do this on his own.

As he got out of the truck, he glanced over the tidy flower beds and mowed lawn, to the building in progress just past the mobile home. The new house, he guessed.

He walked over the flower-lined path, thinking of the difference between this immaculate place and the overgrown yard he would take over. Not only the yard, but the pastures. The place represented a lot of work. One more week, according to Aria. The title transfer was in its last phases.

Then he could roll up his sleeves and get to work.

But first, this.

He squared his shoulders, added another prayer to the ones he'd been sending out ever since he saw Cole in church this morning.

You can do this. You're not some hesitant teen trying to talk to a man you worshipped. Whose opinion you deeply valued.

This visit was a mere courtesy. No matter what came of it, he was still proposing to Aria.

After he bought the ring he'd had his eye on for a couple of weeks.

For the briefest of moments, he slowed his steps, as if unsure of the journey he was beginning. But thoughts of Aria propelled him forward.

Just as he came to the door, it burst open, and Fenna stood in the opening, grinning at him, her ruffled blue dress highlighting the color of her eyes, setting off the flaxen blonde of the single braid flowing over her shoulder. "Hello, Mr. Lucas. Glad you are here."

Her formal greeting made him smile. Fenna had been born in the Netherlands and moved to Aspen Valley when she was seven, and her sweet voice still held traces of a Dutch accent.

"I'm glad I'm here, too," he said, feeling like he should shake her hand.

"Come in. Mom and Dad are in the kitchen. Mom says she's nervous, but Dad said she doesn't need to worry." Fenna shrugged as she stepped aside for him to come in. "I'm not worried."

That Courtney seemed to feel the same jitters encouraged him. Somewhat.

"I'm glad to hear that," he told her, tugging his boots off and setting them beside the neat row of footwear in the entrance.

Cole entered the main living area just as Fenna escorted Lucas inside.

He was wiping his hands on a towel, his expression serious as he glanced Lucas up and down.

"Welcome," he said. "Please sit down. What do you prefer? Tea or coffee?"

"Coffee would be great. Black."

"Be right back."

Lucas glanced around the immaculate living room, shoving his hands into his pockets, not sure what to do.

Fenna dropped onto a recliner, folding her long legs under her. "Just sit down. Make yourself at home."

Again, this made him smile. It was as if the young girl had googled "Proper Things To Say to A Guest" and was now parroting them.

"How is your day going?" she asked as he followed through on her suggestion.

"Quite well. And yours?"

"It's good. I enjoyed church. Did you?"

"I did." This was true, though it would have been more enjoyable if Aria had been there.

"The group sang one of my favorite songs. Did you like the music?"

"Oh, yes."

She fidgeted a moment, as if trying to think of her next rehearsed line, then leaned forward, eyes wide. "My dad thinks you're going to marry Aunt Aria. Is that true?"

Guess she was going off script now.

"Well, I don't want to spoil a surprise. So, I guess you'll have to wait and see." He gave her a wink just as Courtney came into the room, carrying a tray holding mugs and a plate of squares and cookies.

"Welcome, Lucas. Nice to have you here." Courtney set the tray down on the table. "I hope Fenna hasn't been too nosy?" Courtney shot her daughter a warning look, which Fenna shrugged off.

"She's been unfailingly polite," Lucas assured her, stifling a grin.

"Good to hear." Courtney held out a cup of coffee to him, then took one herself, settling onto the couch, Cole joining her.

Though they were all smiling, Lucas felt like he was being interviewed for a job, or worse, interrogated.

"I understand the title transfer is almost complete?" Cole took a brownie and leaned back, taking a bite.

"Yes. Aria said end of this week."

"I'm glad it went so quick."

Lucas nodded, trying not to fidget. He wasn't sure he wanted to say what he needed to in front of Courtney and Fenna, but it seemed they were sticking around.

"Do you have any plans for the place once you take it over?" Courtney asked.

Excellent. Softball question. He could handle that.

"Some. Fencing for sure. I'm hoping we can move some horses from Burke and Karissa's place. Two mares are due to foal, and I'd love to have them close so I can be around when they do, so I can work with them right away."

"You're going to have baby foals, too?" Fenna grinned at him. "We have two now. Mommy and I have been petting them and stroking them." She shot her mother a frown. "What is that called again?"

"Imprinting," Courtney replied.

"Do you do that too?" Fenna asked.

"I try. Haven't done it for a while, so I might have to get some pointers from you and your mother."

"We would be glad to help, wouldn't we?" Fenna turned to her mother.

"Of course we would."

"I understand you breed and train horses here," Lucas said.

"Yes, we do. I've been working on increasing our herd, but so far it keeps me and Hannah Argall busy enough."

Another silence fell, broken only by the clink of Fenna's spoon in her cup as she stirred her tea.

"I understand you wanted to talk to us?" Cole prodded, shooting Lucas a questioning glance.

Okay. This was it.

Lucas pulled in a long breath, sent out another prayer, then put his mug down on the tray, leaning forward. "Yes, I do. I…I want to talk to you about Aria." He cleared his throat. "And me."

"I guessed that from your call the other day."

Courtney's eyes grew wide as she shot a surprised look at Cole. "You said nothing to me about this. We shouldn't be here."

Cole shrugged, his expression serious. "I'm thinking anything Lucas has to say can be said in front of all of us."

With a shake of her head and a roll of her eyes, Courtney stood up. She put her mug on the table beside Cole's, then reached out to Fenna. "Schatje, I want you to come with me to see how the foals are doing."

"But I want to visit with Mr. Lucas."

"Please? Now?"

The firm note in Courtney's voice seemed to be enough to make Fenna blow out her own sigh, put her cup aside, then get up and take her mother's hand. She shot Lucas a parting look and a smile. "Will you be here yet when we're back?"

"I hope so," Lucas assured her. Though he wasn't sure how long it would take him to have his chat with Cole, he didn't think it would take up that much time.

This seemed to satisfy her, and she walked willingly behind her mother as they left.

Cole waited until the door shut behind them, then he took a sip of his coffee, looking over his mug at Lucas. Waiting.

Lucas rubbed his now-damp palms over the legs of his pants. "I know this isn't such an enormous surprise to you, but like you said, I wanted to discuss my relationship with Aria." He swallowed and breathed, trying to steady his now-racing heart. He wasn't sure why he was so nervous. Just that he and Aria hadn't parted on the best of terms the last time they spoke face to face. Though they had texted yesterday, he sensed some reticence. Trouble was he'd already committed to speaking with Cole. Backing out wouldn't look good.

"I got that."

"You know I've always cared about her."

"Even when you broke her heart?"

"I guess I deserve that, though there is more to the story than what you're saying." Not to mention that it was many years ago.

"Aria hinted at something yesterday when we met at the home place, and she shared some…information with me."

Lucas sensed something important had happened then. But he wasn't getting distracted from his current mission.

"You can judge me however you want about that time. Just for context, I had the same discussion with your father that I hope to have now with you. He didn't think I could provide for Aria the way she should be. Trouble was, I believed he was correct. That I didn't have the right to court Aria. I knew I couldn't give her all that he did –"

"No one could. He gave her everything."

Again, that note of bitter anger.

Part of Lucas wanted to follow that up, but Cole's relationship with Aria wasn't his concern.

Yet.

"At the time, I believed your father's words about my position in life and what I could give Aria. But thankfully, time and maturity and confidence helped me see I do have something to give her. A lot in fact. Plus, my feelings for Aria never changed. I loved her then, and I love her now. But this time, I'm not asking permission to marry her. Aria can make her own mind up about how that would work. But I want to have your blessing."

Cole rested his ankle on his knee, folding his hands over his chest. Not the most approachable look, but Lucas didn't back down or look away.

"I know Aria loves you, too," Cole finally responded. "I

think she always has. Though I have to confess I was ticked with you when you broke up with her. She was very hurt."

"I know she was." Despite knowing how it had all come down, Lucas couldn't stifle a shiver of anxiety at Cole's words.

"I know you don't need me to approve or disapprove of your relationship with Aria," Cole said, "But I understand your need for a blessing from me."

Lucas sensed he had something else to say, and just waited.

"I'm going to say straight out, that my dad might be right."

"Right about what?"

"That you don't deserve Aria."

"Who of us ever deserved the person we get in our life?" Lucas returned.

Cole tweaked out a small grin. "Touché," he replied. "I guess I'm saying what I did, because like you said, I don't feel like I deserve Courtney either. There was a time when we had our own difficulties," he said.

Again, Lucas discerned a subtext to the conversation, but he wasn't following that rabbit trail.

"I know better than you that I don't deserve Aria," he returned. "But I also know that she cares for me. I know I'm not the perfect person for her, but I know we belong together. I am still hoping to receive your blessing."

Cole was quiet for a moment, then he nodded. "Of course. If you and Aria get married, you'll be family. I want us to get along. Though I'm sure we'll have differing opinions…" Cole paused, frowning, and apprehension shivered through Lucas.

"Please don't tell me you're a Flames fan," he joked, trying to shift the tone of the conversation.

Thankfully, Cole laughed. "Nothing as serious as that."

"Why do I have a hunch you want to tell me something else?" Lucas asked.

Cole gave him a level look, his eyes seeming to bore into

Lucas. "Are you sure you want to know?"

Lucas held his gaze, determined not to back down.

"I'm thinking not," he admitted. "But if things go the way I hope, we'll be family. If there's some deep, dark secret lurking in the background, I want it out now rather than later. So, if you don't mind telling me, I'd like to get whatever is on your mind, out of the way."

Cole waved off his comments with a flick of his hand. "I wish it was as simple as that."

"Secrets seldom are." He let the comment lay between them as Cole's gaze drifted away, his expression shifting.

"You and my father were quite close," Cole finally began.

Lucas wasn't sure where he was going, but he was willing to play along for now, so he nodded.

"Trouble is, you and I have a completely different view of what my father was like," Cole continued, a faraway tone in his voice. "And you may as well know, that might end up causing some problems. Because of me. Because of you. Because of Aria."

Cole stopped, massaged his temples, then abruptly surged to his feet.

"Sorry. I'm not ready to do this."

And then, without another word, he strode out of the room.

His departure was so abrupt, Lucas wasn't sure what was going on until Cole closed the door behind him, the thump echoing through the room with a sense of finality.

Now what was he supposed to do? He stood to leave just as the door opened again, and Courtney entered the room. She gave Lucas an apologetic look. "I just ran into Cole. He looked upset."

"I have no idea what set him off." He shrugged his uncertainty. "I came here to ask for his blessing on me and Aria. We got to talking about his father, and he stormed out of here."

Courtney pressed her lips together, glancing back over her

shoulder as a sigh drifted out of her. "You may as well sit down again," she told Lucas. "I believe there is something you need to know, and something I feel you haven't heard before. This might take some time."

"I'm sure there's lots I haven't heard before, but unless you can tell me exactly what is going on, I'm leaving too." Then he caught himself. Lifting his hand in a gesture of apology. "I'm sorry. I shouldn't be frustrated, but I am. I wanted to talk to Cole about Aria, and something set him off. Aria's been cagey lately as well. It's tiring."

"He didn't say no to your question, did he?"

"No, and to be perfectly blunt, I don't feel he had the right to," Lucas returned. "I just wanted his blessing, and I think I got it. Though I'm not sure."

"My apologies. This family's dynamics are, well, complicated." Courtney paused, folding and unfolding her hands, fidgeting. She eased out a slow sigh as she held his gaze. "I'm not sure how to tell this to you, but I'm sensing you're tired of the vagueness of this conversation. I may as well come right out and say it. Cole and his father never got along. In fact, Steven Waldren abused Cole."

Lucas frowned, trying to absorb what she had just said. "Abused Cole? As in physically? Verbally?"

"Yes to both."

For a beat, he could only stare at her. Then, when the words registered, they were like a hard punch to the gut. As if someone took his head and twisted it one-eighty degrees.

Simultaneously.

"I can see this would be a shock to you," Courtney continued. "I know you respected and admired Aria's father."

"I did," was all Lucas could manage, shaking his head as if to rearrange the thoughts, sorting through his confusion. "He was like a mentor to me."

"I understand your bewilderment. While he wasn't exactly a mentor to me, Steven was willing to help me out financially at one time when I wanted to train barrel racing horses. It caused tension between me and Cole that I didn't understand, either."

Lucas was surprised to hear this, but again, turned back to what he needed to know. "Did you know about this abuse when you and Cole were dating?"

Courtney gave a vague wave of her hand. "Not directly, no, but his father's treatment was one of the reasons he broke up with me when we were younger."

"How so?"

"Cole had a temper. For the most part, he kept it under control. But his dad was ragging on him more and more. Growing more emotionally abusive, then physically. One night, at a party, all the pressure and anger got to Cole. He beat up a guy who had been flirting with Aria and wouldn't leave her alone. It was bad, and a huge turning point for him. He was terrified that he was turning into his father. Thankfully, the boy didn't press charges. I think he was afraid of Cole's father, too. But he said goodbye to me via an email, and I heard nothing more from him until I returned from the Netherlands to see my father. During that time, Cole and I reconnected. He finally told me the truth about our breakup. As a couple, we're good, but I know he's still dealing with the repercussions of his father's treatment."

"How long did his father...abuse him?" Lucas couldn't help his stumble. He knew neither Courtney nor Cole would lie about this, but it was such a stretch for him to shift his opinion of Steven to include this information.

"I don't know it all. Cole prefers not to talk about it much, but I believe it started in high school. Cole was a mouthy kid and started pushing back against his father. He knew Aria was getting preferential treatment. Trouble was, Aria didn't know the extent of what their father was doing to Cole."

"That's hardly her fault," Lucas couldn't help putting in.

"I'm not saying it was," Courtney agreed. "She was young,

and at that age kids are self-involved. Her life was going well. How could Cole's not be the same? But the discrepancy between the two of them was growing, and Cole was getting angrier."

"Why would Steven be like that?"

"I don't know. The only thing Cole and I could come up with was that perhaps Aria reminded Steven of his wife. Despite how he behaved to Cole, he loved Aria dearly."

Lucas' mind drifted to the letters Aria had found. How they had affected her. But that was for another conversation.

"When did Aria find out about her father and Cole?" he asked. "Did she ever figure it out on her own?"

"Not the extent of it. She overheard some of the fights, but whenever she tried to ask Cole about it, he would brush it off. So, it's not all on her. Cole wanted nobody, especially her, to know. He was ashamed of the hold his father had over him. Ashamed of what had happened to him. It wasn't until Steven was dead that he felt a measure of freedom and space to say anything to Aria about it. And by that time, you were also out of her life."

Again, Lucas felt like he was drowning in information, trying to keep his head above water. "I'm sorry… but I can't wrap my head around this."

Courtney gave him an encouraging smile. "Of course not. I understand that your relationship with Steven was vastly different from that of Cole's. Even that of Aria's. And the trouble is that the difference between Cole and Aria's memories of their father are also disparate. It's created a dissonance between them and a lot of guilt on Aria's part. She shared that you had some information about Steven's childhood. That he had been abused as well."

"Yes. I thought Aria and Cole knew that."

"This family is as bad as mine when it comes to secrets," Courtney sighed.

Lucas sat back in the chair, dragging his hands over his

face, as if pulling all the information down into one place. Trying to let it gel.

"I knew Steven had a temper. I saw bits and pieces of it at times. But I never knew… I never thought…

"And that's what makes things difficult for Cole. The extreme juxtaposition of character for everyone, not only in his family but also in the community. Their father was a well-respected man, both in the community and in church. That's another reason Cole kept this to himself; he doubted he would be believed. But Cole became the target of all his father's repressed anger. Now that we know about Cole's father, I'm thinking a lot of that repressed anger stemmed from Steven's relationship with his own father."

Lucas shook his head slowly. "But… But that's no excuse," he fumbled around, trying to find the right words to say.

His hands tingled, and his palms felt slick. He recognized the symptoms. The same ones he often got after watching video of his rides, seeing how close he had come a couple times to debilitating injury, maybe even death, as horse hooves flashed out within inches of his face. Something he didn't see until afterward.

He felt like that now. Little glimpses he had gotten of Steven's anger. Anger he had dismissed or targeted to his own behavior and failings. Now he realized that they were part and parcel of who Steven was.

Then ice slithered through his veins. "Did he ever do anything to Aria?"

"I doubt it. Aria was always his golden girl. I think she reminded him of his wife. And from what I understood, he worshiped her." Courtney lifted her shoulders in a shrug. "Who knows? He's not here to explain or defend himself. Not that I could listen to any defense he might have. I know what he did to my husband."

How could he have been so blind? How he could not have seen this in a man he thought he knew and wanted to be like?

A man he had at one time respected. Looked up to. Worshiped almost.

Questions and concerns swirled through his brain, his head aching with the pressure of it all.

"So Aria didn't know this about her father while we were dating?"

Courtney shook her head. "Not as far as I know. I think she had some inkling. I've heard her talking with Cole about times that their father was angry. Times that he would lose his temper. But all of us deal with that. I know your father was a kind and caring man, but I'm sure you had your moments with him, too."

"Of course. I was hardly the perfect son. I got grounded more times than I want to think about. There were times I wanted to run away from home. When I wished I had another father." He shook his head. "Trouble is, the man I sometimes thought I wanted as my father instead was Aria's dad."

"I'm sure this will take time for you to process."

"You think?" Then Lucas gave her an apologetic look. "I'm sorry. I shouldn't be sarcastic. But you're right. However, I feel like… I feel like I have no right to face either Cole or Aria. I feel like I've taken a part of their father that they never had. I feel unworthy of all that."

He stood, shoving one hand into his pocket, his other raking through his hair.

Courtney came to stand beside him. She laid a gentle hand on his shoulder. "You don't need to apologize for what you had with their father. That was not your choice or your doing. That's all on him. I hope you don't take this on. I hope you don't end up feeling guilty about all of this."

Lucas looked down at her, thankful for her support, yet knowing, despite her kind words, that he would feel exactly what she had told him not to.

Guilt. Regret.

Fury.

Chapter 14

"Where is Lucas?" Aria asked, glancing around as they gathered for the dress rehearsal. She'd been waiting for half an hour for him to come in the door, but he hadn't shown up.

She had texted him on her way back from Calgary to tell him the news about her new partner, Drew. She thought he would be excited to know that she might have more free time. Though she hoped he wouldn't think anything about the fact that she and Drew had once dated.

When she called him, he hadn't answered. All she had gotten in response to her text was a generic thumbs up, and one happy face emoji. Not even the one with heart eyes.

Hardly communicative.

What could've happened between then and now? Was he still upset with her when she walked away from him the other day?

She knew they had to talk about what he had told her. She had already discussed it with Cole, but now she and Lucas needed to straighten a few things out. But how could they do that if he wouldn't reply to her? She had hoped that tonight, after the practice, they could talk.

She had called Cole to see how he was doing. He wasn't any more open than Lucas was. All she got was a noncommittal, "I'm fine. Still processing, but it's all gonna be okay."

Not exactly negative, but not much for her to work with.

Honestly, the men in her life were harder to deal with than a hostile witness.

Hostile she could deal with, but this was passive retreat. This borderline ghosting infuriated her.

She looked around again as the door opened and Grady walked in. He gave her a sheepish look, holding a rolled-up script in his hand.

He walked up to Aria. "I guess I'm doing this part for now. Again."

Aria frowned at him. "What do you mean?"

She was about to ask him more when Courtney bustled up. She rested a hand on Aria's shoulder, giving her a light squeeze of assurance.

"Lucas called me and said he couldn't make it to the practice. Grady just came back, and Lucas asked if could take over for now."

"Please define 'for now?'" Aria struggled to keep the frustration out of her voice.

"Don't worry, it will be fine."

But the frown marring Courtney's face told Aria a different story. She didn't know about "fine." She wanted to know what was happening.

But people were already taking their places, and she knew she wouldn't discover anything right now.

Grady was fun and engaging, but he was no Lucas. And there was no way she was kissing this man at the end. Thankfully, they were only focused on the first half of the play. By the time they got to the kiss, she was sure Lucas would be back.

When the rehearsal was over, she texted Lucas, but again, no answer.

At the end of the week, he would have to come to her office to sign off on the final sale documents. The handing over of the ranch and the end of a legacy.

Cole would get his money and, hopefully, could turn his back on that part of his life.

But even as she imagined that, she realized the house would still be there.

And she would, hopefully, be living in it.

"Okay, that's enough for tonight," Courtney called out. She looked exhausted, and once again, Aria was worried for her. Wondering if she had taken on too much.

She was about to go talk to her when Brooke caught her by the arm, pulling her aside. She looked tired as well.

"Hey, I need to talk to you."

Aria watched Courtney, who had her back to both of them, leave the hall, Cole by her side. Missed her chance for now.

"What do you need?" Aria asked, shifting her bag on her shoulder.

"So, I have a problem," Brooke said, fingering the tassel on her purse. "Well, it's just…me and Grady…we've been on a couple of dates…and now, well, Gord asked me out. And I don't know what to do."

Aria stifled a twitch of annoyance with her friend.

"Honey, I think you've been hitching your wagon to Gord's star for too long. I think he's only interested because, suddenly, you're not showing up at his diner. You're not as interested in him as you used to be." She quirked a questioning brow at Brooke. "Right?"

"No, I'm not. It's just…what if I'm making a mistake?"

"Mistake? By not letting yourself get caught up in an old habit? By letting Gord decide what will happen and when?" Aria laid her hand on Brooke's shoulder and gave it a light shake. "You know what me and the other gals at Breakfast Club have been saying for a long, long time."

"I know. Forget about Gord. He's not worth it."

"He's known for a long time how you feel about him. But he's done nothing about it. Until Grady shows interest in you."

"Maybe he's shy…"

Aria wanted to give Brooke's shoulder a hard shake. "Maybe he's just an idiot playing dog in the manger. Don't let him get to you. Put yourself first."

"You're right. I think mooning over Gord is just a bad habit."

"There's nothing wrong with liking someone, but that someone needs to deserve you."

Her words resonated, reminding her of what her father had said to Lucas.

"And you think Grady does?"

"I think Grady has been waiting for you to pull your head out of the clouds, and when you started pulling away from Gord, he took his chance. Which, to me, shows what a great and considerate guy he is."

"He is pretty sweet," Brooke shared, a faint flush tingeing her cheek. Then she gave Aria a pained look. "I'm not being wishy washy, am I? Liking Gord so long, then moving onto Grady?"

This time Aria gave her friend's shoulder a shake. "Girl, you don't know the meaning of wishy washy. There's a ton of other women in this town that I would call that, but you are not one of them. By any stretch."

Brooke gave her a warm smile. "Thanks for the pep talk. I knew I could count on you."

"What are friends for but to keep each other accountable and, sometimes, give each other a shake."

Then Brooke's expression shifted, and she frowned. "So, where was Lucas tonight?"

Aria stifled another frustrated sigh. "I don't know. I tried to text and call him, but he's not picking up."

"He's not ghosting you again, is he?"

Her innocent words peeled back the layers Aria had formed over her basic insecurity when it came to Lucas. Insecurity that bothered her but also made her realize how much this man had always meant to her.

"No, I don't think so." She injected a tone of bravado into her voice, forced a broad smile. "He's probably busy."

"Burke was here," her friend suggested.

"Well, maybe Lucas is covering for his brother." Aria made a show of looking at her watch, the universal signal for "time to go." Then she hurried, "Sorry, hon, I've got a bunch of work to do before Drew arrives."

"Oh, yeah. I heard he might come back here. That's cool that it's a go." Then her expression grew serious. "So, you and Drew used to date. Do you think that's why Lucas –"

"No, not at all." She waved off the question before Brooke could finish. "Fun fact, it was Lucas who suggested I hire Drew."

"I know, but still, now that's a reality…" Brooke's voice trailed off, taking along every doubt and insecurity that Aria had struggled with since Lucas left her the first time.

She pulled in a deep breath, reminding herself that she was her own person. An independent woman.

That what was going on with Lucas was something easily explainable. She knew how he felt about her, knew how she felt about him.

And if he was having second thoughts?

She straightened her shoulders, lifted her head, and held Brooke's questioning gaze.

"Whatever happens will happen. I'm not worrying about it."

Brave words, and she hoped she could take them to heart.

But as she walked back to her car, her mind wandered back to the many times Lucas would accompany her. The kisses they shared.

Her firm stride faltered for a moment, then she caught herself and once again straightened her shoulders. She wasn't letting Lucas get to her. If he wasn't talking to her, well, she wasn't chasing after him.

She had her pride, after all.

But as she drove away, that pride seemed like a ragged comfort.

"LUCAS, WE NEED TO TALK."

Burke took the paintbrush Lucas was wielding and set it aside on the paint can.

They were working on the final sets for the play in the shop on the farm, since the hall was running out of space.

"What about?"

Burke hoisted himself up on the workbench of the shop, his elbows resting on his knees as he leaned forward.

"About how weird you've been the past few days. You haven't come to rehearsals, which messes things up for everyone else. And you've been out riding fence on the Waldren place, but you didn't take fencing supplies with you."

"The fences are good."

"Then why ride them?"

Lucas wished his brother would leave him alone. He was still sorting out his emotions, his reaction to what Courtney had told him. "It's something to do," was his feeble defense.

"There's no lack of work here, you know. We've got a couple of hay binds that need some maintenance, and once that's done, you can probably do a cut of hay off one of the fields at the Waldren ranch."

"It's not mine yet."

"Yet. But come Friday, it will be. May as well be ready to cut as soon as that happens."

Lucas scraped his hand over his chin, avoiding Burke's

penetrating look. He'd been on the receiving end of those looks all week. Ever since he skipped church and then a couple of rehearsals. He couldn't face Aria yet. Or even think about what to say to Cole.

"So, what's going on? Tell Uncle Burke."

His brother's patronizing tone grated.

"Don't want to talk about it yet." He was still processing it all.

"Okay, fair enough. I know the girls are wondering what's going on. Aria didn't show up to Breakfast Club yesterday, and that's not like her."

"Well, they can wonder for a while too."

"Celeste is coming home next week. I know she was thrilled to know that you and Aria were back together."

"What are you saying?"

Burke shrugged. "I'm sure the girls have been keeping her up to date. And you know Celeste."

All too well.

Shelby and Karissa he could handle. But Celeste? She had always been a force to be reckoned with. Whenever she came into the room, it was like a whirlwind had arrived. With her flashing green eyes, auburn hair, and sassy attitude, she more than made up for the fact that she was five years younger and about a foot shorter.

In fact, she had texted him yesterday to tell him she needed to have a "chat" with him when she arrived.

No thanks.

"It's not just some simple disagreement," Lucas began, mentally sorting through the things he wanted to say. "It's bigger than that."

"So start small."

"There's nothing 'small' about this all." He released a harsh laugh.

Burke said nothing, just waited.

"You know how much I admired Steven Waldren, right?"

This was greeted with a curt nod. Lucas knew Burke had viewed the relationship as disloyal to their father.

"So, last week I went to Cole and Courtney's to talk to Cole about…about asking his blessing on mine and Aria's relationship."

"That didn't go well for you the last time you did that with Aria's father."

"I wasn't asking for permission this time. Just a blessing as a way of easing things between me and Cole. I knew he thought little of me when I took off on Aria all those years ago."

"Cole said no?"

"He didn't. He just started talking about our differing views of his father and then suddenly left, saying he wasn't ready to do this."

"And 'this' being?"

Lucas dragged in a ragged breath. "Courtney came back, and she filled me in. Apparently, the man I admired so much and wanted to emulate abused Cole. Physically. Verbally."

"What? Really?"

The surprise on his brother's face, the shock in his voice, felt like vindication for Lucas' own reaction.

"Yes. Really."

"How come…he never…we didn't…" Burke looked as perplexed as Lucas had been.

"I understood from Courtney that shame was part of Cole's secrecy. His dad was well respected in the community, so he didn't think anyone would believe him. I mean, look at how we responded to that."

Burke shook his head, looking down, a frown furrowing his forehead. "I believe him, but it's hard to put it all together."

"That's where things get difficult. Because my relationship with Steven, and Aria's as well, were so different from Cole's relationship with his father. I can't stop feeling guilty about that. Like I said to Courtney, I feel like I had a part of their father that Cole never had."

"He didn't do anything to Aria, did he?"

"No. She was the golden child. They figure she reminded Steven of his wife. I know he spoiled her. That car he gave her after I broke up with her was a stark reminder of what I could give her compared to what she'd been used to."

"I can see that you need time for all of this, but is it fair to Aria to keep her in the dark?"

"No, it isn't. I know that, but I have no idea what to say to her. The way I was always spouting off about her father and how wonderful he was, and then to find this out."

"Are you embarrassed?"

"I wish it was only that. I'm ashamed."

"You didn't know. That's not on you. That's on Mr. Waldren."

"My rational brain says that's true, but the part of me that loves Aria and wants Cole's blessing feels like it's an immense problem. I want to become a part of their family."

"Why not ask Aria what she thinks? How she feels?"

Lucas was silent and got a level look from Burke.

"You need to get this sorted out," Burke pressed. "Retreating from the problem only makes it worse."

"I'm not retreating," Lucas protested. "I'm just trying to get my head wrapped around it all."

"On your own. Without the help of the woman you want to marry."

When he put it that way, it did sound selfish. Inconsiderate.

"But what do I say to her?"

Burke pushed away from the counter and walked over to Lucas' side. "Hey. I understand that this is hard for you. But if there's one thing I learned in my relationship with Karissa, it's that you need to be upfront with everything. Everything you think and feel. No secrets. Just tell her what you told me. Tell her how you feel."

Lucas only nodded, wishing it was that easy.

"Trust me. You're not doing your relationship any favors by keeping all this to yourself," Burke continued.

Then the door of the shop opened, and Roxie and RayAnn came in, looking expectantly from brother to brother. "You guys look serious. What's going on?" Roxie asked.

"Nothing," they both said at once.

Roxie gave RayAnn a knowing look. "I'm thinking we should have shown up earlier. We might have found out why Lucas hasn't been at rehearsals."

"I'm thinking you girls are too nosy for your own good." Lucas shot them a mocking look. "All done with community service?"

The smugness dropped off their faces, and RayAnn nodded. "Yeah, though Grady miffed his lines so much that Courtney made us stay longer." She glared at Lucas. "Lucas, you've got to come back. There's no way Grady can replace you."

"He wasn't supposed to."

"Aria's been looking grumpy, too." Roxie sighed. "Seriously, whatever it is you two fought about, could you just settle it already? It's messing up the whole play. Why don't I just call Aria, and you two can talk to each other?" Roxie pulled out her phone, but Lucas waved her off.

"You two have enough going on that you don't need to stick your nose into my business," Lucas admonished.

Then, with another glance at his brother, he turned and left.

He knew what he had to do. He just had to figure out how to make it work.

Chapter 15

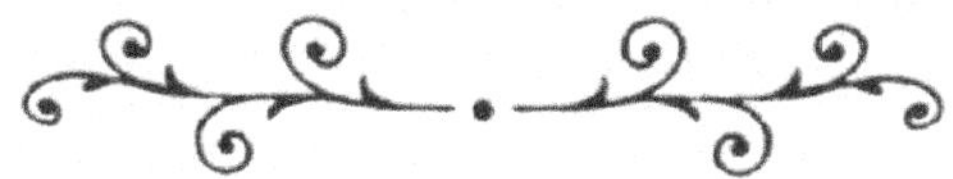

"I'm glad you took the time to come," Aria told Drew as she led him back into her office. "I know it's quite a shift for you, coming to this small practice from the city, so this probably helps a bit."

"It's exactly the shift I've been looking for," Drew responded, slipping his hands in the pockets of his blue jeans and smiling as he looked around her office. "I need to slow down. Make a life for myself."

"Aspen Valley is a good place," Aria agreed. "Good community and lots going on."

"I hear a play is in the works. A western retelling of Pride and Prejudice."

Aria nodded, glancing down at the file on her desk. The final papers for the transfer of title lay inside. All she needed was to get Lucas to sign the papers, and they could finalize the sale.

She had thought Cole would be happier about the news when she told him, but he had been almost ambivalent about it all.

In fact, he had gone as dark as Lucas had. Aria had asked

Courtney what was going on, but all she would say was that Aria should talk to Lucas.

"Yes. Another month and I think it'll be ready to present to the public."

"And you and Lucas are the Miss Bennet and Mr. Darcy?"

"Objection. Leading."

"It's a simple yes or no question."

"Which you know the answer to," Aria replied, forcing a smile. Her emotions had been so in flux over the past while. Humor was getting harder and harder to find. As was patience. She knew Grady wasn't taking over for Lucas, but he had missed the last three rehearsals. Time was ticking.

In more ways than one. Each time Grady showed up, she grew angrier.

And she wasn't sitting around, waiting anymore.

In fact, once Drew was gone, she was heading to Burke and Karissa's place to not only give Lucas the papers but also to confront him about what was going on.

If he was changing his mind about them, she needed to know from him directly. None of this going quiet and letting her draw her own conclusions.

"So, is there anything else you need to know?" Aria asked, fingering the file folder.

"No, I think we've got it all covered."

"Good. I'll get Freya to draw up the Partnership Agreement. You can look it over. Have someone at your firm vet it and give you any advice you might need."

"I'm not worried. I think we can make this work."

He gave her a gentle smile, which hearkened back to the time they were dating. They'd had fun together, but had both realized theirs was a more platonic relationship.

"Excellent." She reached out her hand, and he took it between both of his as he gave it a light squeeze. "I look forward to having someone helping me out."

"I'm glad about that. You look like you could use the help."

"Is it the multiple piles of files on the floor that was your first clue?"

Drew chuckled, still holding her hand, but then he grew serious. "That and the fact that you look weary. Drawn. Tired."

"You know those are not words a woman likes to hear."

Drew shrugged. "I think we know each other well enough that I can be honest with you."

She smiled at that, pulling her hand away from his. "I am tired and worn out."

"And not just from work?"

The tone in his voice told her that he seemed to know what else was happening.

"Already plugged into the Aspen Valley chit chat?" she teased.

"Had a bite to eat at Gord's cafe. The Coffin Cheaters were out in full force. I heard a few things."

Aria just groaned. Goodness knows how those old guys found stuff out, but somehow they each knew someone who knew something, and when they put their grizzled heads together, all the pieces of whatever they were puzzling out would fit together.

Or they would just draw their own conclusions.

"I'm not asking what you heard because it's probably exaggerated and wrong."

"Are you and Lucas okay?"

Aria knew she couldn't dodge anymore.

"I don't know what we are. He suddenly went weird. About the same time my brother Cole did."

"Did they have a fight? Is that why Lucas has retreated?"

That he even knew that much should bother her, but she knew she had to brush it off. It was true, after all.

"Neither of them are talking to me, and I'm getting annoyed."

"And afraid, maybe?"

There it was. The old insecurity that she had felt the first time Lucas had left was now creeping around the edges of her mind, making her resentful and annoyed.

"Yeah, a bit. Though you are one of the few people I would dare admit that to."

After Lucas left the first time, she had put on a brave face with her friends. But somehow, it was easy to tell Drew how she felt once he realized that she still was hurting from her breakup with Lucas.

"It's not weakness to be afraid."

"No, but it bothers me that I let him have that much hold on me."

"You care about him. Of course, he would have a hold on you. As, I'm sure, you do on him."

As she held his warm gaze, she thought back to what Lucas had told her. How her father had made him feel.

Her father who had abused her brother so badly.

And she had never known the extent of it.

"I'd like to think I do."

Drew released that slow, crooked grin that melted so many hearts, but it only made her smile.

"Of course you do. You're an amazing woman."

"I am, aren't I?"

"Not great with grammar, but amazing in so many other ways."

She chuckled at that, which she guessed was his intent.

"You're a good man, Drew Rozak. I hope someday some woman will see that for herself."

"I'm not looking."

She knew him well enough to hear the faint yearning in his voice. She knew that deep down, he still had feelings for

Lucas's sister, Nadia. Had most of his life. Except she was too flighty. Unsure of what she wanted.

According to Lucas, not much had changed. She was still wandering the world, working to make enough to pay for her next trip to wherever she felt she should go. Aria didn't know what made her so restless, but she wondered if something didn't haunt Nadia as well.

"I know you aren't," she said. "Not right now, anyway."

Drew chuckled at that and gave a shrug.

"Much as I'd love to keep chatting, I should get going. I want to get back to Calgary before I hit rush hour traffic." He grinned. "I won't miss that."

He gave her another smile, then turned and left, closing the door behind him.

Aria stayed standing behind her desk, looking down at the file for the transfer of land. The ranch that held such a variety of memories, shifting into other hands.

Again, a welter of conflicting thoughts washed over her.

But at the same time, she knew what she had to do. She had been moping around long enough. Wondering what Lucas was thinking.

Time to take things in her own hands for a change.

HE SHOULD HAVE GONE STRAIGHT to town, but on impulse he turned into the Waldren driveway.

Correction, Prins driveway?

Would he ever be able to think of this as his own?

He drove into the yard, parked the truck, and got out.

It was as if he had to look at the place through different eyes.

But drifting like a wisp of dark smoke through his mind, came the question. How would this all work out for Cole and Aria?

He stood for a moment, sorting his memories. It was still difficult to make the sudden shift from seeing Aria's father as his hero to realizing that he was a horrible person who had done horrible things.

To his own son.

He walked to the house and entered the deck. The house was locked, so he sat on one of the deck chairs, looking out over the yard.

A week ago, he would have felt a surge of pride. Ownership. This place he had so long admired would be his.

His and his family's, he corrected, recognizing that he couldn't have done this without Burke and Shelby's help. Without the ability to borrow against the original farm.

But it was still going to be his home.

And Aria's.

Still would, he hoped. But how was he to view this place now?

How to separate his memories from the ones he was sure Cole still held.

He was about to go back to his truck when the sound of a vehicle snagged his attention.

His heart stuttered when he saw Aria's car coming down the driveway. She pulled up beside his truck and got out, looking around.

When she saw him, she strode over, joining him on the deck.

"What are you doing here?" she asked.

That was the first thing she wanted to know? After what he had done?

He brushed that aside, realizing he had no right to judge her on anything. He was the one who had pulled back from her.

"Trying to figure things out, I guess," he said.

Aria frowned at him, taking a few steps closer. "What things?"

Lucas held her guarded gaze, knowing she had every right to keep herself back from him.

All he wanted to do right now was pull her close and kiss her. Erase the last few days. Erase everything he had learned. Go back to where they were before.

But that was impossible. So much had changed, and yet nothing really had. He still loved her dearly, as he always had.

"I'm sorry. I'm sorry I didn't answer your text. I'm sorry I didn't come to practice. I'm sorry I pushed you away." He knew his apology wouldn't erase the silence he had created between them, but he hoped it would melt a sliver of the ice in her eyes.

She looked away from him, walking toward the railing of the deck.

The silence between them held the weight of everything he had discovered.

"Why did you do it?" she asked. "Why ghost me like that?"

"Because I was afraid. I was confused. But that doesn't excuse what I did. It just explains it."

She shot a frown at him. "Confused and afraid about what?"

"Have you talked to Cole about us? You and me?"

She waved off his question with the disdainful flick of her hand. "He's being as tightlipped as you are, and I'm not gonna lie. I'm sick and tired of the men in my life being such jerks."

He deserved that, though it made him flinch.

"I talked to Cole about us," he told her.

"Why?"

"Because he's your brother, and your only living relative, I wanted to receive his blessing on my relationship with you."

"Why would you need his blessing? Didn't turn out well for me the last time you did that." Then she gave him a sharp look. "Or did it turn out exactly the same, and you just accepted that? I know you're not one of Cole's favorite people."

"No, that wasn't it. And I didn't go to Cole to ask him for his permission. Because he's going to be a part of my life as well, I didn't want any tension between us. I just wanted to let him know what I wanted to do."

Aria gave him a wary look, but he sensed a glimmer of hope in her expression. "What did you want to do?"

Lucas shoved his hand through his hair, thinking of the plans he and the two R's had made. A romantic setting with candles and music playing. The traditional proposal, down on one knee. The box opening to reveal the ring that Shelby had helped him pick out.

But it was out now. May as well go with it.

"I told him that I wanted to marry you." He blew out another sigh. "And this was not how I wanted this to happen."

"Okay, then we'll leave that aside for now. Let's do this one logical step at a time," she responded, her features softening. "What happened when you and Cole spoke?"

She turned, leaning back against the railing behind her, her arms crossed. She tossed her hair back and held his eyes, her gaze steady as she waited.

"Honestly, nothing happened between me and Cole. I talked to him about us, and then we started talking about your dad and my relationship with him. Cole got agitated, stood, said he wasn't ready for this, and stormed out the door. I sat there for a moment, not sure what to do. Courtney entered the room, and she took the time to explain a few things to me."

He stopped there, his gut still churning over what Courtney had told him.

"What did she explain?" Aria prompted into the quiet.

Lucas swallowed down the anger that surged through him.

"I found out about your dad." Another pause to pull his emotions together. "I found out the horrible things he had done to your brother. It spun my world around. It changed everything for me." He swallowed, still struggling with the unexpected surge of guilt he felt every time he thought of his own relationship with Aria and Cole's father. "It was so wrong. So wrong that your father treated me the way he did. And Cole…" His voice trailed off. He couldn't even imagine how it felt for Cole to be on the receiving end of a father's anger. "I thought of all the times I talked to you about your father. How I admired him. How much he did for me. And then to know what he was like to his own son. It's so wrong, and I didn't know. Anything. Did you?"

Aria looked down, as if unable to face him. "I knew bits and pieces. I heard my dad yelling at Cole sometimes, but Cole said nothing to me. Nothing until our dad died. All that time, and he kept it to himself. But the other day…after you talked to him…he showed me…" her voice broke, her shoulders sagged, and her hands flew up, covering her face.

Lucas watched her, then he heard a choked sob.

And he couldn't stay where he was anymore.

He rushed to her side, gathered her into his arms, and held her close. Closing his eyes he pressed his cheek to her head, inhaling the familiar smell of her, his heart breaking at the way her shoulders shook, and her suppressed cries.

He wasn't sure what to say, so he kept quiet, just holding her, thankful she didn't pull away.

He rocked her gently, trying to soothe her. She clung to his shirt, her tears flowing onto it, dampening it.

"Did he do the same thing to you that he did to Cole?" He ground the words out, not sure he was ready to hear what she had to say. Courtney had said he hadn't, but he needed to know for sure.

"No, he didn't," she choked out.

Then her arms slipped around him, and she tucked her head into the crook of his neck, seeking his embrace.

"I never knew how awful it was for him," Aria sobbed. "I

never knew. My dad…he gave me so much. And Cole…" her voice broke on her brother's name.

He tightened his grip on her, letting her release her troubled grief.

He didn't know how long they stood together, but he would hold her until the sun set, if it would give her the comfort she sought from him.

She pulled back, wiping her face, sniffing, and giving him a watery smile. "I must look a mess."

He pulled a handkerchief out of his pocket and handed it to her. She wiped her eyes, blew her nose, and balled up the handkerchief in her hands. She blew out a wavering breath.

"Come and sit down," he offered, moving to the chairs.

She nodded and sank down onto one. He pulled his chair beside hers so he could be as close to her as possible.

Leaning back, she swallowed, looking away from him.

"This is exactly where I sat with Cole when he told me about what dad did." She sniffed, wiped her nose again, then rolled her head to face him. "I can't believe I never knew how bad it was. I can't believe Cole never told me."

"Did you have any inkling? I mean, I'm not trying to say you should have –"

"Don't worry. I feel like I should have too. Probably too self-absorbed. I was getting gifts and attention from dad." She shook her head. "How could I have been so utterly selfish?"

"Did he do things for Cole as well as you?"

"Oh yeah. It wasn't like Cole was starving in a garret while I lived the life of a princess. He and Dad used to go riding lots. I knew Cole was getting groomed to take over the farm. We had a wonderful life at one time. And then it all seemed to fall apart after mom died. We were all grieving in our own way, and the family splintered after that. I got quiet, Cole got rebellious, and Dad got angry. I knew that much about him. But I never knew how bad his anger became. Or how much he and Cole clashed." She gave him a careful smile. "I was always thankful that I had you during that time."

Lucas felt a twist of sorrow, wondering if he had truly been the supportive friend he should have been. Aria talked little about her mother. And Steven had rarely talked much about his wife.

"How did you feel about your father during that time?"

Aria blew out a ragged sigh. "Like I said, I was caught up in my own stuff. You and me. Losing Mom. Dad and I seemed to bond more after that. I heard from people that I reminded him of Mom. So maybe that's why…"

"But how did I fit into all of this?"

"And isn't that the question?" Aria's expression shifted. "I'm guessing it was because you were always way more interested in his rodeo life than Cole was. Cole always resented the times that Dad left the farm, leaving him in charge. Looking back now, that was unfair of…Dad. Cole wasn't that old. Things would break down, and Dad would think Cole should have fixed them." Aria bit her lip, shaking her head. "Trouble is, knowing now what Cole told me, it's like I'm taking the knowledge and filtering my memories through it. And I'm not liking what I see."

"What don't you like?"

"How selfish I was, and how horrible my dad was, and a deep sorrow and frustration that I couldn't see what was going on."

Lucas knew not to give her any platitudes or to assure her she was only behaving like any other teen girl would. At the time, they had been dating as well, so they had both been rather caught up in each other.

Then she shook her head, turning back to him. "And the worst of it is, I still feel like I care for my father. How in the world can I like or care for a man that did that to my brother? How can I love him? It's wrong. It's not right. I can't…..I can't…I know what he did to my brother. I saw the marks.

How can I even think about caring for a monster like that? It makes little sense. I'm just so confused."

The anguish in her voice tormented him, and it seemed to echo his own confused feelings for her father.

Lord, give me some guidance here, he prayed. *Give me wisdom.*

He let the prayer settle, then moved to her chair, kneeling in front of her, taking her chilly hands in his.

"Do you think it was wrong to care for him?"

"I feel like it is. The way he treated me was so unfair compared to how he treated Cole. I know how Cole feels about him, but I also know it's not the same way I have felt about our dad. Am I wrong?"

"I don't know if this is a problem you have to solve or a journey you have to take. He was your father, and I know you're confused about how to remember him."

"But he did horrible things to you, too."

Lucas was quiet for a minute, guilt wavering through him.

"You don't need to take that on. I should have fought harder for you. I should have respected the love we shared. I should have fought and realized that I had put wrong expectations on you. In my mind, you were materialistic and a bit selfish, maybe. I'm so sorry I felt that way. The fact that I left, well, that's not all on your dad. Much as I hate to admit it, that's on me too. I should have just told your dad that I loved you and that we were getting married. Period. I shouldn't have let how I felt about him, and what I had assumed about you, get in the way. I guess I was just afraid he would take everything you had away from you, and that you would resent that."

"I wasn't that shallow."

"No. I know that now, but like I told you before, I felt like I couldn't give you what I thought you deserved as well as what you had grown up with."

"None of us deserves all we have. It's all a gift from God for us to serve him with."

Her wise words settled some of the secondary doubts he felt.

And the irony of her saying this while they sat on the deck of the house belonging to the property he would soon own wasn't lost on him.

She clutched his hands, her smile holding an edge of sorrow and her eyes, confusion.

"I don't think it's ever wrong to love someone. And I don't think it's ever possible to love too much. How you feel about your father and how Cole does, I guess you have to realize you are dealing with two different people with two different memories. It's not wrong, and it's not being unfair or a traitor to Cole to recognize that some of your emotions for your father are legitimate and valid. They're not wrong or right, they just are. You're not asking Cole to feel the way you felt about your father, and I doubt he's doing the same to you."

"I felt like he was last time we talked."

"Or maybe he finally dared tell you what happened to him so you could make up your own mind about your father."

Lucas stood, pulling her to her feet, and enveloped her into a warm hug.

"That's been my struggle as well. Trying to figure out how to feel about your father. Feeling guilty that I received the attention Cole should have gotten. I think I speak for both of us when I say I don't know who he was."

"All the above? None of the above?" Aria leaned back in his arms, looking up at him. "You know, the real irony in all of this is that my father didn't think you were worthy of me. In reality, it was the other way around. He was the unworthy one."

Lucas released a light sigh. "Maybe."

"But you know, I'm tired of talking about my dad," Aria decided. "About the past."

This was his cue.

But he still hesitated to say what burned in his soul. This didn't seem like the time or place.

"I am too," he agreed. "And I want to talk about the future more. Tonight."

He knew the girls would have to do some scrambling to get everything together, but he was determined to do this right. Proper. Romantic.

"Okay…?" she let the word drag out into a question.

He stopped anything else she might have to say with a kiss.

"I'll pick you up at 7:00."

"So, not dinner then?"

He shook his head. He didn't have time for that.

"Nope. And no more questions."

Another kiss, and then he took her hand and led her away from the house to her car.

He waited until she got in and started driving away.

Then he got into his truck, made a few quick phone calls, sent out some rapid texts, and burned out of the yard.

Chapter 16

"We tried our best," Roxie said, frowning as she inspected the set they had created in one corner of the hall. "I'm not sure…"

"It looks amazing," Lucas assured her.

His family had all pitched in and set up the living room set of the play in the hall. They swathed parts of it in glittery fabric, put out the table, and placed candles wherever there was a spot for one. Mini lights draped over the top of the entire background, creating a soft glow enhanced by the candles.

Sparkly fabric draped a table which held a plethora of candles, and two wine glasses flanked a bouquet of pink roses. A bottle of wine lay nestled in a bucket of ice beside the table.

"How come you never proposed to me like this?" Karissa joked, nudging Burke.

"Hey, at great personal cost to my physical health, I painted our names on the railroad bridge."

Karissa chuckled at that. "And I get to see it every time I go to town."

"I'm surprised it hasn't been painted over yet," Klint

commented, brushing some glitter off his pants. "Seriously, why so much sparkle?"

"It was on the fabric and fell off while we were working with it," RayAnn responded, giving him a flick of her hand. "We got it from Karissa's shop, so blame her."

"I've got all the candles put up and turned on," Jacob put in, joining them. "Why didn't you use real ones?"

"Because by the time we lit them all, the first ones would be burnt down already."

"The last thing we need is to destroy all these amazing sets that we've spent so much time working on, just so Lucas can propose," Burke noted.

"I think this looks amazing." Shelby stood back, hands resting on her hips, smiling as she looked around the transformed room.

"Cue the music," Roxie called to RayAnn.

Country music by Ian Tyson flowed out from hidden speakers, and Roxie looked to Lucas. "What do you think?"

"You guys did an amazing job. I love the artist you chose."

"We all know he's your favorite."

"Country with class," he rejoined, shaking his head at all that his family had come together to do for him.

And for Aria.

He looked over the set one more time, a slow curl of apprehension spinning through his stomach.

"You look nervous," Klint teased. "Scared she'll say no?"

So much had been dumped on both of them during the past week, which made Lucas wonder.

"Or worse, maybe." Burke clapped his hand on his brother's shoulder. "I don't think you need to worry too much. It will all be fine."

Fine was optimistic. Lucas knew that he and Aria would have their challenges. He hadn't spoken to Cole since that truncated conversation that hadn't ended well. He knew that Aria and Cole were close…

"Well, I better go and get the potential bride to be," Karissa declared, giving Lucas an encouraging smile.

Initially Lucas had planned on picking her up, but Karissa nixed that. She said she would pick her up so that Lucas could wait for her. Ready.

But now, Lucas wasn't sure that was such a good idea. He'd be standing here, waiting, wondering…

"I'll stick around until Karissa texts me that all is going to plan," Burke assured him.

"I'll be fine. You can go." He preferred to be alone. Preferred to go over what he wanted to say without his brother distracting him.

"You sure? Last chance," Burke teased.

Lucas just nodded, rubbed his icily damp palms over his pants and sent up another of many, many prayers.

Then, as his family left, he started to pace.

KARISSA PULLED up to the hall and put her car in park.

"Well, Cinderella, this is as far as this pumpkin is taking you."

Aria gave her a curious smile, the thrum of anxiety that began when her friend came to get her, only increasing as they drove. Karissa had called her earlier this evening, telling her to clear her schedule and get ready for a drive.

When Karissa picked her up, she wouldn't say where they were going. Though Aria had a rough idea because of what Lucas said, she didn't know how far to follow her racing imagination and glimmering hope.

The only thing she got from Karissa was bits and bobs of gossip, both local and family. A few single girls' hearts were fluttering at the thought of Drew Rozak coming back to Aspen Valley. Celeste said she was making her way home as well.

Aria played along and asked about Nadia. Though she was three years younger, when Aria had been dating Lucas, there was always something about the reclusive girl that drew her in. Nadia would show Aria paintings she had done that she didn't show anyone else. The girl had an incredible talent, and Aria wondered if she was doing anything with it.

But all thoughts of other Prins family members fled when she glimpsed Lucas' truck parked around the side of the hall.

He was here.

And it didn't look like Karissa was sticking around.

"Take care, my dear," was all Karissa would say, adding a quick grin as Aria got out of the car.

As she left, Aria hesitated a moment, giving herself a critical once over. White sandals, flowing grey pants, silky pink top. Scarf instead of necklaces. Too dressy?

Not dressy enough?

"You don't even know what's happening," she told herself, straightening her shoulders, tossing her hair back, clutching her bag with one hand, and striding up the walk, then the stairs, before yanking the door open.

Country music drifted around the darkened hall. She caught the glow of light and turned toward it.

Then gasped.

Lucas stood by the table of the set of the drawing room from the play. Candles glowed, mini lights twinkled, and the music created a fitting counterpoint to the western look of the set.

She swallowed as she and Lucas looked across the room at each other.

Then, suddenly, they were both walking toward each other, slowly at first, then faster.

They met halfway, and as he pulled her into his arms, she wrapped hers around him. Their mouths met. Hungry, yearning.

As if the separation and misunderstandings of the past

few days hadn't happened. As if it was all swept away by their embrace.

Moments later, they pulled apart.

Lucas stepped aside and led her to the table, gesturing to the chair.

Aria took a moment to appreciate the setting and all the work that had gone into making it so romantic.

"This is incredible," she told him, as she sat.

"You are incredible."

She gave him a dry look, and he answered with a shrug. "It was waiting to be said."

He fidgeted a moment, then put his hand in his pocket. "I have something I want to ask you," he said, as he went down on one knee, pulling a ring out. It sparkled in the low light, sending out rainbow rays of light, refracting the glow of the candles.

Aria's breath caught in her throat. She had guessed this would happen, and yet she felt surprised. Amazed and yet feeling a sense of utter rightness.

"Aria Waldren, I love you. I always have," he began, holding up the ring. He looked from her to it, then back again. "I don't know how else to say this, but I want to marry you, and I hope you feel the same."

She felt a surprising knot of tears tighten her throat. Then, all she could do was pull him close, give him a tight hug, then draw back.

"I do feel the same. I do want to marry you."

He blew out a breath, as if he had been holding it, waiting for her reply. Then he slipped the ring onto her finger, pushing it over her knuckle. He lifted her hand, twisting it back and forth, letting the light play over it.

She looked down at the simple, square-cut diamond, unable to keep the smile off her face.

"It's beautiful," she smiled. "It's almost as perfect as you."

He chuckled, holding her hand, then stood, pulling her up close to him.

"I think that's supposed to be my line."

"You can't come up with all the corny stuff. I'm allowed a few, too."

He looked down into her eyes, their gazes meshing.

"I love you so much," he murmured, his voice breaking a little. "I've been so foolish to let you go. To leave you hanging. I've made so many mistakes."

She placed a gentle finger on his lips, letting it linger, then tracing their outline. "We aren't talking about the past right now. We'll have enough to deal with later. This is just about us, right?"

"You're right," he whispered. Then pulled her close. Kissed her again.

A while later, they pulled back, wanting to prolong the moment.

Aria held her hand up again, the diamond shooting out rays of refracted light. "It's so beautiful."

"You mean that?"

"I do. But you know, it could be a ring pop, and I would have been just as happy."

"Really?" Lucas shook his head. "Could have saved myself some money had I known that."

"Of course, it wouldn't last as long."

He chuckled, gave her another kiss, and then stepped away. "You know, I could do this all night, but there are a few people who I know desperately want to know how this story ended."

Aria smiled back, then waved her hand around the set. "Well, they all know how this particular story ended."

"Yes, and I'm not letting Grady usurp my role."

"I think he would only be too happy to let you take it back." She stroked his cheek, just because.

He caught her hand and pressed a kiss to her palm, curling his fingers around it.

"We're going to do great. I just know it."

"I do, too. We've been through a lot to get here, but we made it. And we have each other, our family, our faith, and the community to help us through whatever comes next."

"Amen to that," he agreed with a smile.

IF YOU ENJOYED GETTING to know Lucas and Aira then check out the next book in the series, meet the next sibling of the family - Celeste in A Loving Heart.

Should she have come here alone?

Celeste wrapped her hands around the leather cover of the steering wheel of her inappropriate sports car, chewing on the inside of her cheek as she looked over the mess in front of her.

Rows of rusted automobiles and tractors were parked haphazardly along a jagged treeline. An enormous pile of peeled logs hulked beside them. Appliances, old bathtubs, and boxes of unknown items lay strewn in front of the vehicles and the logs, grass growing up between it all.

The perfect place for a murder and endless places to stash a body.

Lucas told her that the place Wade Hicks had taken over was not only an eyesore but a hazard. His father was a hoarder who didn't see a box of junk at an auction he didn't think was precious. Or a car he could do something with.

And apparently, along with the log-home building business Wade had inherited, had come his father's stash. However, she didn't need to wander through the cluttered yard.

She just needed to talk to the guy she now saw striding across the yard, hefting a piece of lumber.

Celeste paused a moment, watching him, sifting back through her memories. Wade and his family had lived in Aspen Valley until he was sixteen and Celeste remembered Wade too well. He had been four years ahead of her in school, and his quiet and serious demeanor held a curious appeal.

And she had an outsize crush on him. If her brothers had known, they would have taunted and teased her endlessly.

As they did with any guy she started dating when she turned sixteen.

But now Wade Hicks was back in Aspen Valley. The skinny teenager had filled out, but he was still lean and muscular. Three days' worth of scruff accented his narrow features. He looked hard and tough.

And even more crush-worthy, as RayAnn would say. Not that Celeste was looking. She only needed one thing from Wade Hicks. And that was his log-building expertise.

As she got out of the car, he turned toward her, still holding the piece of wood, and she had to suppress a gasp. Bright red blood drifted from a wound on his temple, accentuating an expression that shifted from grim to grimmer at the sight of her.

"Help you?" he called out.

Man of few words. Again, she'd been warned.

"I hope you can," she said, plastering on her best, *'have I got a deal for you'* smile as she walked toward him.

He kept staring at her, his eyes like chips of ice fringed with dark lashes, his blonde hair falling over his forehead, framing his forbidding features.

"I don't know if you remember me, but I'm Celeste Prins. We went to school together."

He frowned, still said nothing. Still looked at her like he wished she were gone.

But she wasn't allowing herself to be fazed by his antagonism. Maybe he was just tired. Maybe she caught him at the wrong time. She hadn't scrabbled her way through the thickets of the financial world by being put off by antagonistic males.

"I also heard that you moved back here not that long ago either," she continued, twisting her mouth into a polite smile. Wondering if she should point out the blood on his forehead.

Maybe not.

His only reply was to lower the piece of lumber to the ground, still supporting it with his gloved hands.

How could this guy keep this up? Even the most hardened CEO's said something by this time.

Never mind. She was here on a mission and wasn't leaving until she got what she wanted.

"My brothers told me you build log homes. Like your father and uncle did."

This netted her a quick nod.

"Burke, Lucas, Liam are my brothers in case you didn't know," she continued. "I believe you went to school with them as well."

He doesn't need your family bio. Zip it.

And her bright chatting didn't get her anything more than a blink of his eyes.

"Anyhow, I heard you and Vince Kaplan were continuing your father's log-home business," she continued, trying not to feel intimidated by the man. "And I would like to hire you to build a log home for me."

Wade set the board down, looking at her as if he was trying to figure her out.

"Can't do it."

"Just like that?"

"Yeah. Just like that."

His sentences grew longer, but his glower was growing deeper. What was with the guy? It was like he disliked her on sight.

Not something she was used to.

Instead, she tossed her head, determined not to be back down. "I know you're busy with the cabins for Walter Crawford, but I was hoping you could build my house after that." It wasn't an ideal situation, but she could wait. For now, she was living at the main house with Burke, Karissa and the siblings that still lived at home, Rayann, Roxie, and Jacob. It was a chance for her to get her feet under her and get caught up with the family and all things Aspen Valley. She'd been living away so long, it would take time for that all to happen.

Besides, Karissa didn't mind the help in the house.

But Wade shook his head. "I'm leaving after that job's done."

This surprised her. "I thought you had just come here? Thought you were staying to run your father's business?" At least that's what her brothers and some old friends had told her.

"Heard wrong. I'm leaving."

His terse replies grated on her, but she still held out some hope she could convince him to do the job. She didn't get to the top of her marketing firm by being beaten down by momentary setbacks.

"Leaving? Where are you headed?" If she had more information, she might plead her cause.

But his frown deepened, and she sensed she had stepped over some invisible boundary.

"I was just asking because if you could squeeze working on my house in before you go…" she let the sentence trail off, in the slim hope he would be interested in the job.

"Can't squeeze in building a log house."

"Okay, maybe wrong choice of words." She chuckled, waving her hand as if making her last words disappear. "But could you? Build it? Before you go? It would be on an acreage just down the lake. I bought it from Arnold Whitman."

"Nice place."

It better be, she thought. She paid enough for it. Burke had offered to subdivide an acreage off one of their quarter sections of land, but none of the quarters were on the lake.

Which is exactly what she had always wanted.

"So, you know how amazing a log house would look there," she pressed, taking advantage of his interest.

His expression didn't shift as he shrugged.

"The trees and the opening overlook the water." She figured she may as well carry on while it seemed he was still listening to her. "It would be perfect. And building this house would be good advertising for you. I could get a quality photo made of it you could use on a marketing brochure." She stopped herself knowing she was slipping into the hard sell she used as a last resort at the financial firm she had worked at. Work that had made her enough money to come home to Aspen Valley and settle here.

"Brochure? Marketing?" The harsh tone of his voice revealed what he thought of her suggestion.

Right. This was Aspen Valley. Word of mouth was the biggest advertising tool available to most businesses. That and contributing to any fundraiser, like the upcoming community play, for example. Which she had.

"Anyhow, it would be good word of mouth."

"Don't need it."

"Don't you think your business would benefit from that?"

"My business is sticking around long enough to finish the job my dad started. Then I'm gone."

He was getting positively loquacious; except she wasn't thrilled about what he expounded on.

And the harsh look in his eyes combined with his tone told her there was little wiggle room left for her.

She dug around in her brain, trying to find something, anything, to change his mind. Back to hard sell. She had nothing to lose, it seemed.

"Well, that's too bad. You'll miss out on a chance to build a once-in-a lifetime home. I've got some intriguing ideas for the house. My brother Drake had to cut down this huge elm with branches that have an unbelievable spread that I was going to use as a feature in the main part of the house. We've got the bark peeled, and it's drying. Plus, a fireplace made of river rock we gathered from the Aspen River. The one that flows into the lake."

She caught a faint spark of interest in his eyes, but then he blinked, and it was gone. His gaze swept over her face and once again, his eyes narrowed.

"Gotta get going." He picked up the lumber again and, without another word, he walked away.

It took her a moment to realize what had just happened.

Then Celeste a face at his retreating back.

"Jerk," she muttered.

"Heard that," he called out without turning around, his voice echoing over the yard.

Which didn't help her already hopeless cause.

She flushed but kept her head high, just in case he also

had eyes lurking under that thick mop of tangled hair covering the back of his head.

But he disappeared into another decrepit building.

She waited a few more moments, but then heard a hammer ringing as it pounded nail after nail.

That was that, she realized, huffing her breath out in an exasperated sigh. She spun on the heel of her designer boots and strode back to her car.

As she reversed, she shot another look over the yard. For a moment, she understood why he couldn't help her. Even if he didn't have this other job to do, cleaning up this yard would take months.

But still…she had really hoped to get someone competent to build her house.

And she really wanted Wade Hicks to do it.

A LOVING HEART will be coming out on March 8, 2023

Reader Group

If you want to find out more about me and stay abreast of all my new releases you can sign up for my newsletter by checking out the QR code below. Use your phone to get sent to where you can sign up and get a free book from me as a thank you.

Other Series

I have many other books for you to enjoy. Check them out here.

ASPEN VALLEY ROMANCE

#1 - A Yearning Heart

#2 - A Seeking Heart

#3 - A Loving Heart - March 8, 2023

#4 - A Tender Heart - April 26, 2023

COWBOYS OF ASPEN VALLEY

#1 Western Hearts

#2 Western Wishes

#3 Western Romance

#4 Western Kisses

#5 Western Vows

#6 Western Blessings

ASPEN VALLEY HOMECOMING

#1 The Way Back Home

#2 The Way Back to Faith

#3 The Way Back to Hope

#4 The Way Back to Love